A
Masculine
Trilemma

A novel by Jeffrey Ellinger

Ellinger

For the persecuted

But we are what we are, and we might remember
Not to hate any person, for all are vicious
-Jeffers

I

The Extinction Manual

THE EXTINCTION MANUAL I

I am two fools, I know,
For loving, and for saying so
-Donne

In boyhood, read fantasy.

Cultivate a sensitive personality enthralled with battles happening on an adorable scale where mice travel by sailing on toy-sized wooden ships, and after defeating an evil rabbit they eat feasts of minuscule loaves of bread with bitty hunks of meat that could feed a hundred of their most valiant warriors. These heroic mice drink what would be thimble shots to us but are hefty flagons of elderberry wine and large carafes of honey mead for them.

Think often of being somewhere else, as someone else. While your Mennonite pastor gives sermons on Sunday mornings, draw war battles. Daydream, of an invisible world, hidden in the forest behind your parent's Sears model house, in the heart of the heart of the Great Plains. Grow up far away from literary agents.

Perform adequately in sports. Yearn to be a professional basketball player. Obsess about becoming taller. Once, with your mom in the big city, buy a poster commenting on this dilemma.

'Life is Hard, Play Short,' the poster says, parodying a sneaker slogan. Find comfort in knowing someone, somewhere, understands.

Height is an issue until sophomore year, when you grow, though no longer care as much. You have given up on becoming a basketball player. Desire to be a professional golfer instead.

And be sure, even now as you write this inside Harold for no one, the reason you never made it as a golfer is because you cheated in a regular season tournament, giving yourself a better lie.

A Masculine Trilemma

At regions your senior year you play so poorly, miss the cut for state. Christ saw your cheating, you think now in a study room inside Harold. Christ made you go bald for your boyhood lusts, for wanting *Playboy* playmates with full bushes, sporty women in the swimsuit issues of *Sports Illustrated*.

The literature read in adolescence is the literature assigned by your English teacher, who is your mom. So consider yourself lucky to make friends with Mennonites who attend the private school in your small agrarian town on the plains. Do not drink or have a girlfriend. Contain no direction as a teen other than: 'I'll be a professional golfer. If that doesn't work out, I'll help people.'

Be accepted to a public land grant university. You had wanted to get away from the chew-dipping bros in your class, but money is tight. Think not of a major, so be close, in a desultory sense, to publishing books about your life.

The summer before moving away, Mennonite friends recommend novels about the 'End Times.' You do not like the eschatological work.

'Seems far-fetched,' you say during a book club in the basement of your parents' house.

Do not believe you will be going to hell for being with Ashley, the Mennonite girl you date that last summer. Kiss pink nipples in your parent's basement while *Shawshank Redemption* plays. Decades later, write of kissing 'pink nipples.'

Before leaving home, that last summer, Lacey breaks up with you through a note. Time to store away memorabilia of youth: binders of baseball cards, trophies from playing sports with 12-year-olds, letters from Christian girls met at summer camp, and start a slow march toward your annihilation: of wanting adulation, finding obscurity.

THE EXTINCTION MANUAL II

Virginity is peevish, proud, idle, made of self-love
-Shakespeare

Skip ahead.

Become a middle-aged man who begins artistic projects with no hope for them to be known by anyone outside himself. Contain no learning beyond a bachelor's in psychology from a land grant university on the plains. Hastily, you made your way through higher learning after deciding, too late into your time at the land grant university, you want to be involved in the *creative arts*, somehow.

'But I'm 20 now,' you said to yourself at your land grant university. 'Time start a career, a family.'

Not enough money to restart, you knew then, or the time. You saw yourself as about forty-five. You were twenty.

Decades later, convince yourself you will be successful if you just work hard enough. Believe that, still, alone in a Harold study room, eating breaded chicken bites. Peer to your left, at a cotton-headed woman, plastic covering her head, bending slowly down to browse through a forgotten row of fiction. Look forward to your laptop's screen, knowing the only books left are the books not promoted in end-of-year lists, like *Holy Book*.

A doozy, *Holy Book*, and have trouble now, inside Harold, drumming up the desire to reflect. Say only that *Holy Book* functioned as the foundation for great passions and unanswered queries.

Go back to a most tender age when you read a courtship tract after nearly having sex in a dorm room. The fumbling experience pushes you into anything offering a reason to believe that all impulses are evil, unless one is married, at which point they are ordained and you should be doing them all the time. Pray all the time to a higher power, to give you a partner. Donate spare money to a campus group with weekly meetings where a man who smacks his lips when he prays confirms everything you have been wanting before marriage is bad. Pray hard for someone to marry at a wedding in a church.

The tract outlining your thinking is *I Hugged Courtship Hello.* Written by a home-schooled teen in Oregon, *Hello* features examples of damnation for couples who could not wait on Christ's timing.

With those vestal teachings in mind, after your time at the land grant university, go to your first job in Nebraska, a group home seeking to convert teens to Christ. Fall in love with another houseparent, Elna, who played volleyball for a Christian college in Iowa.

Be crucified as Elna follows *Hugged's* rules with you but tells you late one night in her cottage she did not with her previous boyfriend at the Christian college in Iowa. Long past midnight, on a couch so smooth from years of use, Elna tells you she regrets 'giving away too much' of her body to him.

An anguished year passes. At the end, Elna leaves the group home job three days before she said she would. Crushed by her eluding goodbye, send a mix CD and quilting supplies to her new job at a library in Iowa City. A week later, read her last correspondence. At the end, she writes:

'Please, Henry, stop focusing on me. Focus on Christ. He is the only one who can satisfy your yearnings. It's best we don't talk again.

Sincerely,

Elna.'

Now, after reading that email in your parents' basement on their Gateway computer with the CRT monitor, put your head down on the keyboard. Stay like that for some time.

Look up later and see the gibberish on the screen. Read the symbols, while feeling a hollow ache. Allow this deep pain to fuel you to one day reflect on all this deep pain.

The process, of devastation and recording the devastation, will keep repeating.

THE EXTINCTION MANUAL III

My heart was constricted. I was brushed by a foreboding of truth
- Babel

Once, you extolled *Olympus Ignored*, the objectivist novel recommended to you by Nathan, the managing editor of a Christian music magazine in Texas called *Metal God*. There in Texas you interned, before student-teaching psychology to teens your final semester of college at the land grant university.

One clear memory of that time is of the regular teacher. He reminded you of an actor from a gritty action film from the 70s: kind, with a collection of handguns at home.

The teens you student-teach show you how to twirl your pencil by day. At night, with your aunt in her carpeted apartment, eat Arby's on hard plates while watching the Twins win their only playoff series in the 21st Century. In her extra room, read *Olympus Ignored* and conclude: 'I am reading the only novel that matters.'

Post this revelation on a Dave Matthews Band message board. Ignore the critics who come to the replies. Be sure of everything.

All certainty crumbles in Nebraska. Where Elna, The One who Christ chose for you before making the stars, left the group home without saying. So you quit too, unable to stay in a place where everything spoke her name, the simple ranch houses and quiet roads, even the grass.

Retreat to your parent's house. Enjoy home-cooked meals. Watch professional basketball players fight fans on live television. Play *Sorrowgale*, a fantasy video game. Soon enough, find work in the big city for a package delivery company, overnights at a group home, and an apartment behind

Sunshine Foods. Move in with hand-me-down furniture. Begin to think this thought: *I will be a known artist.*

A deep wanting keeps being thwarted by unseen forces. You want to record that tension. For training, subscribe to an arts magazine, *The Visionary*, based in San Francisco. Start drawing. Try mixing songs. At last, read the graphic novel, *Sweaters.* There, you found it, your inspiration. Begin to write your heartbreak, only to have the first chapter erased when your desktop computer malfunctions. The story, starting with a guy walking in a blizzard to the downtown Sioux Falls library while reflecting on someone named Andromeda, based on Elna, is never recovered.

Quit writing. Focus on *Sorrowgale.* Portable strategy games are for overnight shifts at the group home with a former schoolteacher, Lisa, who sprays you with a water bottle when you fall asleep on the long stretches connecting midnight to dawn. Benevolent grandma is her role, leaving you to discipline children who never had any, or far too much.

In dark stretches connecting the night to morning, read *O Voyagers!*, a novel with the feeling you want to transmit, realistic, using the plains as a canvas. Most of all, browse MySpace, to again find The One.

Meet Susannah, a thrower from Mississippi.

Things go great, for a while, then they fall apart.

To get away from the hurt, move to Cascadia. On the drive west, listen to a philosophy book on CD with a line that explodes your facile faith:

'If it is a miracle God created everything, what a greater miracle if this all happened randomly?'

Driving near Coeur d'Alene, see yourself above your white Taurus, moon higher, black sky littered with white flakes, and think what you think is a deep thought, '*Nature is as much God as there is.*'

Dad warned you not to move, 'just to get away from a heartache.' You insisted, 'That's not what I'm doing, Dad,' though that is what you are doing.

Crossing into Washington, gripping the wheel of your white Taurus, hope that this distance will be enough, remembering how, in your big city studio in McKennan Park, you talked with Susannah every day for two months: about Elna in Nebraska, your virginity, of wanting someone so badly.

And Susannah told you everything too: of an ex at a private college in Georgia with whom she smoked 'dank weed' every day, and a guy in Colorado she didn't consider her second because he only 'put it in and pulled it back out,' and a lot about her first boyfriend in high school, an older guy she met on a mission trip who was the first to 'really pay full attention to my body,' by always starting at her toes and 'not missing a thing' on the way to her head.

Carnal things you learned when you drink with Susannah. Over the phone, drinking orange juice with vodka, a snowstorm battered the plains. A meeting is soon set.

First time in the airport Susannah pops out from behind a potted flower and hugs you. She smells like a fresh garden.

Holding hands to her Jeep, notice the bumper stickers supporting organic food causes. In her rented room inside a mansion, a long kiss and more. *Myspace*, you think, Susannah
finishing in the shower with the detachable head: *Dear Christ, thank you for Myspace.*

Go, over the next two days, to her favorite barbecue restaurant and her Pentecostal church, her family's mansion in the suburbs.

On the final evening, in her small room in a mansion, she straddles you, her silk robe open. A small tuft of hair she trimmed, and you think: *I have found The One.*

So excited about it all, the next morning you do not bother to look up the time of your return flight. Susannah, having no choice that day, takes you to work at her family's organic grocery store. Morning after, in Sioux Falls, a text. Simply a chapter and verse, and the words from her:

'You're just not a strong enough spiritual leader, Henny.'

A friend in Sioux Falls said she planned to move. A commune house in Frellard needed a roommate. So pack up a life into your white Taurus, wave goodbye to your teary mother and stoic father, and drive west to start another life.

THE EXTINCTION MANUAL IV

But try not to bring up *love* so much---it makes you sound like Horace
-Bolano

Surface like a mushroom in fecund Cascadia. Drive with hope to the Industrial District, where you load brown packages into brown trucks. Finish that work at eight in the morning and drive north to Frellard. Stop to get donuts off I-5, at Winchell's. Eat those on the drive through Wallingford. In Frellard, park by the commune house, get out and breathe in the green air. Go in to have cereal. Pour calories down your throat for the energy to clean yachts in the bays and marinas around the city.

Evenings are with volunteer housebuilders from the Middle West. None are in a rush to get married. They all graduated from private colleges and wear skirts with tights underneath. They listen to Cat Power while they whittle wood. Evenings are karaoke and pub trivia with them, weekends of kickball and craft beer, nights of falling into bed with private college graduates from Minnesota and Wisconsin who have moved to Cascadia to save the world by building homes for the dwindling middle class.

First is Hannah. She sleeps on egg-foam in your rented room before your bed arrives in a horse trailer. Then Greer. She rides a longboard to your commune house and has curly hair. Then Elena, an artist from Duluth. She draws birds in her shared house in the Rainier Valley.

One weekend, everyone from Elena's shared house went on hiking trips. Quiet, like a tomb on her lower bunk, Elena takes off her jean skirt, a cotton shirt with little hearts on the floor. The sun goes down as you do everything you had wanted to do back home with The One.

15

Elena rests now, as you in her lower bunk remember smoking a cigarette in college, while waiting in line for tickets to a Sugar Ray concert. The act made you so self-conscious you believed your parents could sense you smoking from a hundred miles away. In Elena's silent room, worries of doom vanish.

Work physical jobs. Go to bed with Christian women. The world is pushing you up, you think after interviewing for a new position at the package delivery company. Visions of financial security fill your mind.

Get the job. Soon wish you had not. Your new boss, Mike, reminds you of Clarvis, from high school, who gave wedgies, laughed at your lisp, and told you more than once, 'If I were her brother, I'd masturbate to thinking about your sister in the shower.'

Greer, Elena, and Hannah get tangled up soon enough. Straighten the amorous cords by breaking up with Hannah one weekend morning. She bikes away more aggressively that morning from your commune house. The next day, with Elena under a tree in an empty park, say you are better off as friends. Elena, always quiet, only agrees, though you can tell, inside her, she does not. Finally, with Greer at Gasworks, explain everything. When you are done she runs away, her sandals flying off.

Find her on a concrete bench. Skyline sparkling against the water, there, on the concrete bench, be forgiven.

Summer ends. One morning, on her way to work at a bike shop in the U-District, Greer flies her fixed gear through the back windshield of a Subaru. That night, go to her at Harborview and see her connected to a sea of wires and tubes. Standing beside her bed, she squeezes your hand. The other women housebuilders are there, but you squeeze back.

Cascadian air becomes colder, wetter. Work on the boats ends. One morning, before driving your white Taurus to the package delivery company, rise with the belief that you must document the heartbreak of Elna, of

Susannah. Write in third person, include diary entries and a lengthy criticism of *I Hugged Courtship Hello*. The pursuit of letters consumes your mornings. In the afternoons and evenings, become a middle-manager dispatcher. At night, visit Greer in the hospital.

One of those nights, bring a new CD by twin Canadian sisters. Greer thanks you with a kiss, her jaw no longer wired shut. Take a walk in the hospital together, stopping on a mezzanine above the cafeteria.

'Thank you,' Greer says. She wears her greenish hospital gown, gray sweatpants, and the sandals that flew off in Gasworks. Her hair is curly. She has green eyes. 'My mom said you've been here every day since the accident. You didn't have to do that, Henry.'

Look down now, at the scattered groups. Peaceful is their communion. Now is the time to explain yourself, to lay yourself prostrate.

'*I was sheltered*,' you think to say. '*That's not an excuse, I know, but I never expected to meet you. That night at Gasworks when I told you about the others, it wasn't enough. You were right to run to the lake. I made things dramatic. I wish I hadn't. I really do.*'

'No problem,' you say.

And as you walk Greer back to her room, the moment is gone. A chance like that, you somehow know, you will not have again.

THE EXTINCTION MANUAL V

You lament the monotony of ass. There's a simple remedy for that—don't avail yourself of it
- Flaubert

Wake up in a commune house in Frellard.

Every morning, keep at it, your big novel about Elna and Susanna and faith and love. Finish that work around noon, drive in your white Taurus to the package delivery company, and be called a 'supervisor,' so your supervisors can have someone to blame when their supervisor comes around. Greer left for college in Bellingham. Stamp down any part of you that says she was The One. That kind of simple thinking was for youth.

At night drink fortified wine and play strip poker with the housebuilders. They have all paired up, except Elena. Do not talk of a relationship. Golf at public courses with Tim and Bill, hike in the Olympic National Forest with Carl and Bethany, flights of craft beer with Lumpy and Tina. Retire in Elena's bed on the weekends. During the week are others. Once, on the way back from camping with Elena and Hannah, receive a text from Lumpy. He is drinking at the housebuilders' haunt, Al's, in Wallingford.

'Rachel, eh?'

Rachel, a new housebuilder, must have shared that you spent the night at her rented house with the backyard chickens. True, the two of you had an evening of red wine, Scrabble and Cat Stevens. Lumpy's text only pains you, rewinding to a party years before, when someone introduced herself by coming right up to you, her hand out, saying: 'Hey, I'm Greer, Pettuur's roommate.'

A joke, the way you pronounced that housebuilder, Peter's, name. So embarrassed by her big hello, Greer turned red and walked to the nearby living room. There she picked up a guitar from a couch and start strumming "The Wind."

A Masculine Trilemma

Never return Lumpy's text.

Go out with new housebuilders, like Monet, recently graduated from the University of North Carolina. Monet wears short black spandex shorts at the weekly frisbee game. Beneath those, in her room in a U-District shared house, are her faded blue underwear. Admire them, looking in a stand-up mirror behind Monet as she works on you. Bill Withers plays.

Drink at night. Write in the morning. Work until evening at the package delivery company. Do not learn to drive a heavy truck with manual transmission. Tell yourself, on commutes in your white Taurus, that's fine. 'Writing' is what will one day keep your belly full.

Elena keeps hers flat through hard work. Fritter that affection away, believing, though you do not want to, that Greer was the one for you. Do not apply for a graduate degree in creative writing.

The commune in Frellard dissolves. Move to Beacon Hill, to the basement of a house owned by an Asian woman who plays online role-playing games, as a job, it seems. Her voice, speaking on the phone with a former literary agent in New York, as you will later learn, seeps through the floorboards.

Go to Elena less in this time. See Wally more. Wally, the guy who loves mid-century novelists, especially Philip Mates. Join Wally in your love of the mid-century man writers, when you should be reading diverse chapbooks, buying them from Tao Himself. At Wally's shared house, meet women recently graduated from private colleges. Like Sammy. She has an eagle flower tattooed on her forearm and journalist parents in Montana. They raised a substantial daughter who stacks books of poetry around her apartment in Capitol Hill, likes sleeping naked and texting things like, 'I wanna feel your cock in my ass.' And Cassie. Back in her Ballard apartment she feeds you microwaved foods, takes hits on her bong, says as she opens her second floor bedroom windows, 'I like it when I know people can hear me.' Meet one with dreads, others from neighborhoods like West Seattle and Ravenna, some who do mushrooms. See as many as you can. Think of it as an accomplishment, to have your body handled by different handlers.

In this time, at a used book sale in a warehouse along Lake Washington, Wally picks up *The Tides* and tells you, book in hand, 'Some people buy their reading for the whole year here today.'

Wally's knowledge of everything and his degree in creative writing makes you trust him, so much you tell him about your novel that same day on the bus ride to his place in Wallingford.

A month or so later, Wally and his poet lover are to review your work. That grey afternoon, right after settling on the floor of his ill-lit bedroom, the poet lover rushes out without saying a thing.

'Most of this isn't working, Henry,' Wally says right away, a stack of your words in his lap, 'but you might be able to salvage an okay short story, after another year or so of editing.'

Try to smile as Wally segues to talking about 'crazy' his poet girlfriend is. Chuckle aloud. On the inside, turn to stone.

After more notes, leave Wally's room, your insides hardened, and walk out to your white Taurus with your marked manuscript, a three-quarter time job at the package delivery company, and on weekends telling people at Wally's house that you have a day job but your passion is, as you tell them, 'Novels, or really what I write are love stories.'

'All stories are love stories,' you say, more than once, as with Amber. Lithe, she asks you one Friday night in Wally's kitchen, her lips tinted purple from wine, 'Are we going to go make out now or what?'

Trail behind Amber to the backyard of that house. Fall together onto wet grass. Fruit crushes beneath you, staining your jeans.

Back inside, everyone left at the party squeezed themselves into the breakfast nook benches etched out in the kitchen.

A Masculine Trilemma

'Why are you two so dirty?' Wally's poet lover asks across from you and Amber. Everyone laughs. The poet lover does not get it, asks again, 'Seriously, why?'

Everyone laughs harder.

Soon is a reading at Wally's. A poster is made, rugs put down, and people you do not know arrive to hear you and Wally and the poet lover read. Another guy from Wally's house recites a poem about how old you are.

'Maybe even 30,' used for a rhyme. Big laughs for that one. No choice, you laugh too.

A week later, on a walk through a forest, to a folk concert with the housebuilders, overhear Rachel call you a *manwhore*.

But the name-calling does not make you want to die in the ditch eating leaves. It gives you a hint of pride.

THE EXTINCTION MANUAL VI

There is turmoil inside me, which seems to ridicule me
-Capitini

With your land grant university degree and a firm belief in Christ you began work at a group home on the stranded plains. There in Nebraska you fell in love with a volleyball player. A year after starting, she left three days earlier than she said she would, so you cried out to Christ but heard nothing.

Long after trying to hear His voice, you live in the basement of a house owned by an Asian woman who plays online video games full-time. She must have sold her shares of Google or Microsoft. Mornings are in her basement, becoming 'a writer,' before walking over I-5 to your real job as a dispatcher at a package delivery company. Nights are with Elena. In the morning, after she leaves to build houses, slip into bed with Hannah across the hall. Every morning Hannah giggles. Gathering her robe, she repeats her line: 'We're being so naughty.'

At the end, stay with Hannah and Elena. You decided you should live closer to home. Nothing left. Greer is not coming back. Your job as the dispatcher is not a world beater.

'I can write anywhere,' you tell yourself one Saturday afternoon in the U-District, looking for solace in a used bookstore. It is not hard to lie to yourself.

In that last month, every night on their secondhand couch, drink cheap wine and watch a British comedy where the main characters speak right into the camera. After the British comedy and the wine, read to Elena and Hannah, stories by the great bisexual, Sleever. By day, sell your possessions, golf clubs, framed art, video games. At night, sleep with Elena. In the morning, fall into Hannah's bed where the earthen redhead shakes. Sunlight crawls into her room one morning as she gets up telling you, 'My, we had a big one this morning.' Sense, watching her leave to the shower, you have been milked.

Another night, after the wine and the British comedy, blanket over the three of you, a hand on each thigh, feel the strong belief flow through their blood. That faith made sense when you moved west, but not anymore, not while striving to become a man who reads important stories that start with: *So help me God it gets more and more preposterous...*

On your last Saturday, alone on the city bus, after pho and browsing used books in the U-District, think of Greer in Bellingham. Watching mossy blocks go by, think of mistakes. Drift off to an unresolved dent on a pickup backed into during your first month in the city. You put a note on the windshield, but the man never called. On the bus, be sure your hair falls out because Fate needs to get even. So unlike Sleever, his biography in your lap, who traveled to Moscow and Rome and Paris to receive awards and at night in Ossining beckoned to have his manhood suckled by young authors. Sleever drank hard liquor until he nearly died but lived long enough for his work to be compiled in a big red book. That night, next to Elena sleeping, thoughts of yearning do not relent.

Later, married and living in a duplex in the cheesy suburbs, you are before a long wooden table as your wife works. That morning, you took a bus through the rusted city, to an interview at a coffee roaster near the deep cold lake.

It's okay, you thought during the interview. *These people probably don't notice my age.*
One, the Administrative Coordinator, is like a busty secretary from a Mates novel. 'Her eyes slip toward the torpedoes pushing out of her encased top,' you think to later write. The Retail Operations Manager, with mounds of hair in a messy bun and a small nose ring, asks a question for the group: 'What's an example of when you had to pay attention to detail at your last job?'

Another applicant fields it as you daydream.

Out through the glass wall of the conference room is a guy sitting inside artful walls, not even a cubicle, who never had to answer that question. Friends with the owners of the coffee roaster, he must drive to work in a Jeep, and his job is to flirt with the interns. He waves his hand and they come.

The interview ends. You get the job, though it does not last.

Now back to when Hannah and Elena waved goodbye. Drive to the frozen suburbs of Minneapolis and live with an old friend slash new landlord, in his attic. On that first night, he, and another guy you did not know would be living in the basement, work on an electric car in the garage while you, in the attic, put away your things, a suit, some clothes, a few books.

Autumn light filters through gauze curtains in your rented attic. On your mattress on the floor, read the screenplay Mates wrote for Styron. Read, after walking to a thrift store in Bloomington. Your new housemate in the basement and your new landlord, who you met in Colorado while proselytizing, looked at you queerly when you told them you planned to walk to the thrift store, miles away in Bloomington. And they were right. It was strange to be on the sidewalk, with pickups and semis zooming by. You wanted to live in the city, but you had no money from your time as a dispatch supervisor.

So now you have walked beside hot traffic. Sunshine moves into your rented attic. Peek through the curtains, at the squat houses, and think of making a dating profile. Everything is moving toward the eventuality, you pretend to feel, toward the ending promised to everyone who has dreams and works hard.

THE EXTINCTION MANUAL VII

This desire to be loved does not amount to a psychosis
- Hubbard

Often in your rented attic, read novels of autobiographical fiction. Not 'autofiction,' not yet are they called that, so they are not bad.

One morning in this solipsistic time, get in your new car, parked in the driveway of that house in the frozen suburbs, and head to a temp agency in a monolithic building in the western suburbs of Minneapolis. Do there what your father warned you against doing, park too far forward in your new Malibu, scraping the front bumper against the curb.

Doesn't bother me, you tell yourself, going in wearing business casual, though it does.

Go give the temp agency manager your resume. Soon get matched with a job at a factory in Crystal, packaging generic pharmaceuticals.

I don't belong, you tell yourself, surrounded by white walls and worn-down workers in white coats, though you do, as well as anyone.

Every morning, after adding quotes from your favorite novelists and screenshots of *MeInMyPlace* photos of models to your personal website (where you embed your novel *Lovers of Salvation*, with a cover of a Bible verse overlaid on a nude woman) drive your new Malibu, with scratches below the front bumper, to the factory. In the locker room, dress in a lab coat, steel-toe boots, a beard net, and walk out to the gleaming white floors and white walls, and be paired up with Rose, who is older, with caked-on makeup. She lashes out at anyone less powerful than her.

At lunch break in the evening, over vending machine sandwiches and soda, check your personal website's stats. Believe progress is made via traffic from snickering old friends. Winter comes. Online date.

25

Meet Claire. She offers to show you around your new freezing city. Decline, thinking one must not accept the first offer, as if you are a businessman doing a deal. Then Maple, who worked at an advertising agency in Portland. In her brick apartment's living room, watch Maple walk nude through lamplight. Think she looks like a Greek goddess. Next is a college student, with black tattoos. She drives to your rented attic at three in the morning. Read to her the Mates novel, *The Christmas Pageant,* on your mattress on the floor. After the reading, she takes off her wool tights, grabs the part of her she bragged about over chat, and asks, 'Do you like it?' Then, Ali, the Muslim film student from Canada with Iranian parents. After a few dates Ali tells you she has another for, as she says over chat, 'carefree fucking.' Then is pancakes with Hannah, the Jewish artist, one snowy morning before packaging generic pharmaceuticals. Hannah kisses you on your landlord's red couch then drives away to Home Depot to pick up supplies for her art installation that will complete her graduate degree. Then Halsey, after Hannah. On I-35, to meet up for pho in Uptown, your Malibu plows through the powder of a new storm. After pho, Halsey invites you over to her nearby place for hookah. Always remember her white underwear, with red hearts. Hours later, drive back on the interstate, packed with wet snow. Something in your Malibu's alignment freezes, and for a long time try to have the issue fixed. Bring it in to various mechanics throughout Southtown. Never find the solution.

Always there is the rented attic, with the low-hanging ceiling fan and the mattress on the floor that belonged to your landlord who has turned into someone looking to be known in Silicon Valley, as you want to be glorified in Brooklyn, with bylines in Important Journals like *Goat Dunker.* Up in that rented attic, submit. Over and over, submit. Keep going with your sad trying, and with Hannah. Winter turns to spring, to summer.

A Masculine Trilemma

One weekend afternoon, after a day at one of the lakes, Hannah naps on the red couch, her legs over your lap. Housemates gone, turn the television to a drama with erotic nuns. They inspire you to do what Hannah asked. Her fantasy, she told you, is to wake up with you in her mouth.

A couple of weeks later, on your mattress on the floor, Hannah tells you to come inside her.

'I'm on the pill,' she says before you begin.

A week later, watching a movie on your laptop in the attic, Hannah hits pause, says in her droll way, 'I'm pregnant.' Silence. Not even the sound of traffic in the frozen suburbs.

'I'm joking,' she says with a tiny smirk, starts the movie again, and you crack a nervous laugh.

A month later, after Thai food on a rainy afternoon before packaging drugs, go to Hannah's shared artist house, to her top floor where it is always hot. Cooler after dousing rains, sit in Hannah's chair, before her slanted table. Nearby is Hannah's shelf that she filled with colorful knick-knacks. Hannah goes and retrieves from her closet the thing she always promised she would show you, and now she is grinning more than you have ever seen her grin, holding the orange dildo. She puts it down, walks over, and pushes down her skirt. She is giving. You are thankful.

'See you later,' she says after at her bedroom door. It is raining. A kiss and leave for work. That evening is a text. Hannah found your dating profile you promised you would delete.

See Hannah once more, by accident, along the Mississippi River. Use that moment for the ending of your online dating novel.

Quit the generic pharmaceutical job. Start work at a corporate bookstore five blocks from your landlord's house in Southtown. Think of selling your tainted Malibu and living in the rented attic, immersing yourself

27

in library books, 'learning what I would have learned at graduate school anyway,' as you tell your landlord once, as he codes on the red couch.

Hot summer ends. Work at the corporate bookstore, not as a bookseller but in the back, with the receiving manager. Hannah's sleuthing freed you, you think as you stack books, like when you moved away from housebuilder gossip about you and Elena in Cascadia.

Meet women in the city just finished with private college. Have them over to your mattress on the floor. See yourself, as your newest sleeps, selling your Malibu and living the transcendentalist lifestyle, becoming known as the Important Creatives in Uptown who must blog for a living. In that time is Harper, a future lawyer. Tell her over pho you work at a bookstore. 'But really,' you say, going up with her to pay, 'I'm a writer.'

And still after private college in St. Paul Harper walks with you out to the parking lot. Be glad to live in the guts of a capitalist society, as your Malibu seems fine to her, even if you know it is defective. Harper follows you in her Volkswagen to the frozen suburbs.

Up in your rented attic, love her 'nipples like thimbles,' as you describe in your novel about online dating. Harper rests her warm head on your chest. Think, *I must shed myself of these attachments.*

The world is romance.

Read *A Game and A Leisure* by Mark Pepper, the Jewish novelist, one weekend morning. Experience what you will describe in your online dating novel, not set in Paris, like Pepper's book, but in brick apartment buildings across Uptown and Seward, or in the frozen suburbs, in your rented attic, after you have turned on your space heater an hour before a date arrives.

You met Harper, the future lawyer. Her stomach had a gentle curve. A runner in college, she gained healthy fat in the year after graduating private college in St. Paul. She held your hand in public places, but you let it go for an aspiring singer, Oceana, who rides you 'like a bull rider,' as you write in dating novel, on her creaky bed in Uptown. Her one room is sectioned off by French doors. One night, hear drunkards hollering in her Uptown streets, then a voice, closer. It is Oceana.

'Fuck you for coming,' you hear. Look over and see Oceana pulling over the blanket to her side of the single bed.

Weeks later, as a way of making up, receive naked pictures to your flip phone. Oceana does not want you to go but off you go. To Aaliyah, who boasts over texts about her 'crazy big ass.' She tells you she sent pictures of it to guys in America, from Thailand, where she worked after her final semester of private college in Northfield. Meet.

For drinks and laughs and more boasting. In the booth of a Nordeast dive bar Aaliyah wraps her scarf around your neck. Hours later, park by her brother's house. In the back seat of your blemished Malibu, Aaliyah puts her warm mouth around you as light snow falls. The holy act over, Aaliyah tells you about her work at a coffee shop in Uptown. You do not care. With Aaliyah touching your hairy thigh, you think you love Aaliyah.

That weekend is karaoke at Vegas Lounge. On the same night, Aaliyah on your mattress on the floor, breath in her strong body.

In the morning, she calls her bestie. She talks into her first iPhone but looks at you on the mattress as she says, 'I don't do butt stuff on the second date. *I'm a lady.*'

Everything is laughter, the best of times.

One day later, Aaliyah texts that she has gone out with another for: 'Fun, young, sweaty things.'

In the attic, drink vodka. Drink and write a blog post about finding and losing love. Hours go by like this. Walk drunk down the carpeted stairs to the kitchen for more. Out in the living room your landlord codes on the red couch, a yellow cat nestled between his outstretched legs on the coffee table. Pour another glass with ice, take a big drink, and as you stumble back up the stairs text a regretful truth from your flip phone: 'You're awfully cavalier with love, aren't you?'

Do not see, or hear, from Aaliyah again.

THE EXTINCTION MANUAL VIII

> But he was not buried in Minneapolis
> At least
> And no more may I be
> Please God
> *-Wright*

Not yet.

Not yet do you know of live-in boyfriends on the first floor of a crumbling duplex, feral men in pajama pants with the distant stare of someone that would hump a sack of flour, if the sack of flour were dense and warm enough. You have not yet heard their animal noises, so you are *naive*. You do not want to die.

In a rented attic of the frozen suburbs of Minneapolis, you want to live. The programmer housemates went away to Silicon Valley for the summer. Your landlord accepted your offer of mowing the yard, looking over everything, so quit your job at the corporate bookstore, and for sustenance eat ramen. Each morning in your rented attic write your novel about online dating and be positive, after finishing another daily goal of 3000 words and readying yourself for your daily jog, *this* will be what brings you the renown you have craved since you started remembering everything about Elna, Susannah, The One. Meet others.

A dancer arrives to the frozen suburbs with a bottle Jameson. Below her bellybutton is a black tattoo: 'EVERYDAY IM HUSTLIN.' Another night, a private college graduate arrives with freckles and eats her grilled hamburger as she tells you about a 'hot Australian' she loved for the last year. After beers, as the orange sets, standing by her scrappy car, she promises the fireworks she brought will be for another time. Watch her drive away for good. Days later, an owner of a flower shop in the North Loop comes down in her Range Rover. A week later, read her text: 'You should perhaps put your eggs in another basket.' Begin to worry you might be defective, in an irreparable way.

Your landlord returns from California in the fall. The other coder from the basement is not back, still on a road trip across the American Southwest. When he returns, he moves out, and you would too, live in Uptown like your dream, but money is low. Pare your novel every morning, assured you are creating a commodifiable work. No one cared about the bildungsroman embedded in your personal website. Everyone has online dated. And this will be a *real novel*, you tell yourself, not some *blog post*.

Winter approaches. Edit in the morning. Run every afternoon in a haunted park behind the Southtown YMCA. Come back to the house and grill for online dates in the evening. No real wanting occurs.

Holidays come. After many submissions to your one Important Creative contact, be accepted to write about popular music for *Sin*. Previous submissions to the culture website were 'like hitting the side of a barn with a bazooka.' Finally, your essay is forwarded along, the one about guys with acoustic guitars at parties. Receive a $100 check that so enlivens your spirit you at last tell your dad, a decade since living under his roof, that you want to be a writer.

'Yeah, Bud,' your dad says over the phone. The air is colder, out on the back porch in the frozen suburbs. A trace of snow on the ground. 'That's an awful hard thing to do.'

The dissuading does not stop you. Go inside and happily invite your landlord to Spirit Sonny's, a dive bar in Uptown. Celebratory drinks, cheap appetizers.

Everything is great, you think as you toast.

Freelance checks do not sustain you, so find a job at a steelyard in North Minneapolis, an apartment in the upper level of a duplex in Nordeast. Days are cutting steel, nights are in front of a computer screen. Sometimes, so exhausted after the steelyard and a long hot shower, fall asleep on your mattress, no longer on the floor. Extra money is for cheap liquor to help you network with Important Creatives online. One will be the key to the life of having ideas and writing them for money, you are sure.

More than anything, you want love. That will not change.

'The longing never goes away,' as the Southern novelist, Mercy, once wrote. Maintain the notion you still hold an appeal for a certain kind of woman, one with a larger than average nose who never played sports in high school and now hula-hoops as her fitness activity.

Look for her, work at the steelyard, start to blog for *Feeling Magazine* where, as they once said in their about page, 'All feelings are relevant.' Months of uploading there before an email from a producer who offers you a position to write 'full-time.'

'Yes!' You reply on your phone in the dirty breakroom at the steelyard, thinking that blogging 'full-time' (without pay) will get you something. With tenacity go to your new position of unpaid blogger every night after work.

One crisp Sunday, bike to a coffee shop in St. Paul. Meet up with your former boss from the corporate bookstore where you unloaded boxes in the backroom.

'It's a *human* novel,' your former manager tells you over his tea. 'But I will need more time to digest it.'

Offer a revised draft.

'Yes, of course,' your former manager says, but without energy. Take back the manuscript with fake confidence. Leave, not much later, with a firm handshake and a thank you.

Cycling back along the Mississippi River, tattered manuscript in your messenger bag, know that if your manager had loved what he read, he would have been more enthusiastic, like when he talked about going to Pearl Jam concerts. Over fifty he had been to.

Doesn't matter, you think as you bike, going fast down a hill, a part of you wanting to fall off the bike and die, the other part wanting to keep trying, to keep going and one day *be known,* by oceans, as Vedder.

Feeling Magazine at night, steelyard by day, weekends are unenthusiastic dates. Upload a post in this repeating time about your most popular post, 'What My Dating Profile Would Look Like, If I Were Honest.'

From its wake, gain female followers from across the world. In direct messages, see smiling faces. Appreciate barest portraits, from Minnesota to Canada to Tennessee.

Cut steel, every day dreaming of becoming an Important Creative in Uptown. Believe it all might be happening. A woman of important standing messages you over social media, invites you to the dive bar near your place in Nordeast. Barely a drink in, confuse her alma mater with a similar university.

'It's *Wellesley*, not *Wesley*,' she says, bristling in her booth. The whole evening is bristling. Leave, not even a full drink later, with a stale hug, and bike to the duplex alone. Never hear from the Important Creative again.

Begin to see Unity, a journalist for a small newspaper outside of the city. Commiserate about the insularity of the Important Creatives in Minneapolis. One of Unity's essays, written under an alias for *Quadrangle*, the local status blog, commented on what it was like to be in a submissive-dominant relationship, the one she is in with you, you learn. The article received no promotion on the website's social media.

'Doesn't seem fair to me either,' you say to her one weekend morning, wishing Unity would concentrate on editing your online dating novel. It is late morning and has smoked. She lowers her head.

After she is finished with her loud work, she gives you a kiss on the cheek, gets up to shower. Walking away, notice once more how Unity's form, tanlined from a trip to Jamaica with her parents. For a moment, care less about your dreams.

They can be distractions from a better reality, you try to believe as you turn on the TV, hearing the running water of the shower.

Only a night later (Unity is never invited over two nights in a row), come across the dating profile of another Important Creative. In her profile she includes a link to her fiction, as you do in yours. Wake the next morning for the steelyard. Reach down to the wood floor for your phone to see a message from her. Your heart beats fast against your chest as you read:

'I like your writing. We should talk over beers.'

Go out for margaritas, for tacos on Eat Street. Smoke American Spirits with her, though you do not smoke. After drinks and telling this blonde Important Creative, a basketball star in her small hometown in Minnesota, your certain belief, 'I could beat up 99.9% of all living American male writers,' walk to her place along the interstate for pizza and a black and white movie. In her room, a single framed photo on her wall of a writer you do not know but are too proud to ask who it is, receive her significant backside, like an athlete's, not a fey writer.

Early in the morning, at her rainbow stickered front door's threshold, she whispers, 'Talk soon.' Leave her building near the interstate with a lightness so thrilling you are inspired to text her the next day, a Sunday: 'We should hang tonight.'

'I have pages,' she replies.

Whatever *pages* are you are sure they are important. Text again the next day. Receive nothing in response.

You must be in love again, as you are the one who waits. Not a French philosopher, you are a laborer who believes he needs more social media followers if he is ever going to make it.

THE EXTINCTION MANUAL IX

Writing is the least ascetic of all actions
-Cioran

Fly to a wedding in the South. Meet someone uninterested in her status online. Walk down the aisle with her.

After the ceremony, the sun sets along a marsh next to a former plantation house with pillars. Drink champagne on the grass. She cries when she laughs.

This is the last person I will be with, you think, smoking hand-rolled cigars, drinking free liquor. A band with a horn section plays. Everyone is ebullient on the dance floor under old, heavy trees.

Next morning at brunch, the groom hands you a note. The one you walked down the aisle with is sad you never came out to the bar, where her and the groom talked about how you had *good meat.*

Later that day, help the newly married couple open presents, heavy envelopes. Dinner is leftover sandwiches, and the groom gives you a number, tells you to text her about how you spent the day 'eating meat sandwiches.'

'She'll think it's funny,' he says, giggling.

Press send while admiring a waitress in a Southern bar who the groom says is, 'Nice, dang.' The bride just rolls her eyes. For the previous year the groom has been in residence, sleeping with women in Chicago, while his betrothed organized their event in the South.

A meeting is set in Tomah. Do not close everything. Another time, in the Dells, take laps in the hotel pool, between each one take, a big drink from a glass of whiskey she holds. In rural Wisconsin, your relationship grows.

Invite your new lady to Nordeast where you live above two Minnesota graduates who are, according to the realtor who showed you the duplex, 'Cute as a button.' Invite your new lady you walked down the aisle with but know you also want the Minnesota graduates to want you. As a dead writer, if that is what it takes, at the bottom of the frozen Mississippi River.

Alive with the one you wooed with talk of meat sandwiches, drive to the Sculpture Garden, to your pho place against The Greenway, to the gingerbread lane of houses in Seward, ask her how old she is and if she likes Drake. These are all your old tricks. They work fine enough.

Fine enough that for a week in her brick apartment along a deep cold lake you sit at her kitchen table as you write about emotions, while she works at her real job at a hospital. Upload those 'articles,' as you call them, to *Feeling Magazine*'s servers. Receive no promotion. While your new lady works in the afternoon, read *The Starving Beast*, the novel by the famous Bill Zucker, and again later do the same, recently in La Crosse, after transitioning into a married man who accepts old friends to stay at a brick apartment shared with his new lady who was so upset her man did not have the sense to tell those former Christian friends to get a hotel for a locally-sourced food convention she talks about kicking you out, and what then?

Back to Sioux Falls, most likely, hoping there to meet a creature like the one Bill Zucker dreamed of coming on and writing about his coming on, though a Cuban graduate student, like in *The Starving Beast,* would not be in Sioux Falls. The available ones are too young for you to seriously entertain now.

During your first visit, drive your car to a used bookstore in the beer-soaked town where the only customer is a homeless man talking to himself about Satan. Take a paperback copy of *The Starving Beast* to the counter, where the worker wears a no-frills dress and looks down as you buy the book, embarrassed to know what it is in the male brain. Nod goodbye, taking with you a copy of another man's fantasies, and go out into rusted city. During that visit, discuss moving in together.

Go to Minneapolis, quit the steelyard, work two weeks, and drive back to your lady's place by the deep cold lake.

First thing, sign up for an exercise class. In the dark silence of early morning sweat on black mats in a building of new condominiums. Heave next to college girls who must be glad to have their lithe boyfriends.

Back in the brick apartment, while your new lady does real work at a hospital, search for fake jobs, like deejay at a radio station. Write a cover letter, referencing your time as the music director at your college radio station, a decade prior.

All jobs are stopgaps, you think as you hit apply. Writing for a living is still your hope. How that can ever happen, you are unsure, as *Feeling Magazine's* editors are nonplussed to your work, even to your list with one thousand bullet points to which you only receive an email from a producer, who says, 'Thanks for the list!'

Your lady soon offers an idea, one that would have occurred to you, had you not been so obsessed with becoming known: Go back to school for 'something practical,' like English teacher.

You do not tell her 'That is the last job I want.' You do not say 'I really want to teach college girls philosophical novels, and for them to think I am *sensitive and deep.*'

You do say, one night in the brick apartment, after giving in to the idea, 'Everyone will see me and think: That guy has no idea what he wants.'

'I know what I want,' you do not say. 'I just have no idea how to get it.'

THE EXTINCTION MANUAL X

Let those I love try to forgive
what I have made
-Pound

Attend two classes at a university along the deep cold lake to attain a degree to teach English to teens. Quit before a week passes, after a summer of acquiring signatures, loan paperwork, transcripts. Begin work at a social services agency in West Allis.

Drive around the rusted city. Interview women whose grandparents fled the South for a better life. Now those women take care of abandoned children.

Instead of writing of their struggles, journal in the brick apartment, before your lady comes from the hospital, about being unconnected to Important Creatives. Your lady will be a physician.

'He's a freelance writer,' you imagine her telling confused colleagues.

One ostracized afternoon, compose your final article for *Feeling Magazine*. Following its posting, nothing.

Every day, drive around the North Side. Interview aunts and grandmas. Social reports about them are for little money. Afternoon is you, alone in the brick apartment. At night, sleep on the couch, after your lady came across pictures of spanked asses in your phone. Think of applying to a graduate program in creative writing.

Make up. Go with your lady west, to Cascadia, and visit old friends. Hannah, the red-haired Christian, visits at the same time. At a Super Bowl party she splays herself on her newest boyfriend, in a way that says to your

39

lady, *Yes I fucked your man, and I fuck other men too, and I will be going to heaven when I die…isn't that great?*

After the Super Bowl party, through the side streets of Ballard, your lady yells. If she wants to break up with you, or if all relationships are this pregnant with arguments, you cannot say. This is your first real one.

Back in the rusted city, tension recedes enough for you to concentrate on your new position, assisting a supervisor in the program where social workers venture into the poorest neighborhoods to assess the capabilities of aunts and grandmas to care for grandchildren, nephews, and nieces who otherwise would become wards of the state.

By your new boss, be affectionately nicknamed, 'My little bitch.'

Enter data. Answer the phone. Check paperwork.

If nuclear war is staved, your job will one day be done by artificial intelligence, you are sure.

A small amount of money is made, so little that when you tell your lady one evening how much, she is oddly silent.

Work at your cubicle near the fairgrounds. In the late afternoon, add to your journal. When your lady gets home, the conversation gets to how your former Christian friends were rude. In the morning, drive to a cubicle near the fairgrounds. At night, engage in disagreements in a small brick apartment along the deep cold lake.

To get out of the cycle, go back to the plains. Watch your nephews perform in a school play. One of the musical numbers inspires you to buy an engagement ring.

Drive back to the brick apartment knowing your family will be happy. On previous visits with your lady, they made a bed upstairs and a bed downstairs.

A Masculine Trilemma

Spend an evening at your lady's favorite restaurant. After dinner, drive to a spot overlooking the lake. Darkened mansions on one side, small park on the other, tell her to open the glove compartment.

She takes out a travel book with a bookmark. On its back you have scrawled a quote: *I love you and you are lovely.* Dome light on, reach into your suit pocket and give the modest ring. She weeps.

The next month, go to the courthouse, repeat vows. Married by a justice of the peace, two lawyers witness your union. One cries while filming the proceedings, your wife later says. Rush down a hallway into blinding sunlight. Stand blinking before a fountain as a stranger takes your first picture. Drive to the cubicle that same afternoon. Your wife needs to go back to work at the hospital.

Days later is a trip back home. Eat a catered meal with your family in the fellowship hall of your Mennonite church in the country. Aunts and uncles and some cousins are there. Nothing is like you imagined as a youth, down to the music you curated, playing too softly over dinner. Your wife is pensive.

In the morning, take off for an island. High over the ocean a man makes trouble. Stewards handcuff him, drag him to the back. As a wedding treat, your wife paid extra to be in the front of passenger class. During the flight, the man's drug-induced stumbling plays out right in front of you. As the plane taxis, your new wife does not speak. Something about how she thinks you took the side of the passenger to your left.

'Everything is ruined,' she says in the darkness of the hotel room.

Not a week later, resume work in the cubicle. Confront errors in a self-published novel about online dating, which you read into a camera for an audience you still believe is out there.

Before your lady, your wife, returns to the brick apartment every evening, add to your puerile journal. Advertise your online dating novel to meager followers. Earn a couple likes, one from an Asian millennial in Brooklyn who followed you long ago. She gives a middling score. Sales drip in, a couple from your wife's colleagues at the hospital who do not look in your direction at small plates restaurants. Supply nothing by releasing a book of intimate moments which professional contacts would not broach in a polite dinner where everyone wears pressed jeans and starched blouses from the mall. Wake every day, eat a terse breakfast. Drive on the interstate. Sit in the cubicle. Listen to your boss talk about how she wants 'hard anal' with men who are not her husband. Drive back to the brick apartment. Write your thoughts about the day. Wait for your wife to come home and argue. Walk to the exercise class. Eat a terse dinner. Watch reality television. Retire to bed chastely.

Wake up and do it again.

THE EXTINCTION MANUAL XI

Everything had been transformed into orgasm and visible, chattering oceans of elf language
-McKenna

Bore forward another year. Publish a second self-published book.

Dwindling followers must believe you rushed it, when really your second effort required years alone across the country, in rented rooms, basements, attics, and a brick apartment along a deep cold lake, where you live with a woman who comes home to a husband typing his thoughts. Contain no ability to conjure factions for alien races.

Fly to New Orleans and meet up with friends. A week before, the couple sent a picture of the wife on her knees eating her husband's ass. Judging from your wife's reaction---a night of her crying on a bench overlooking the deep cold lake, telling you she is not trying to be the *cool girl*---you should have known not to comment on the delicate creatures on Bourbon and Chartres.

There, your old friend encourages you, so you do, but you should have known that your wife would not appreciate you leering at the delicate creatures drinking hurricanes and browsing for art. That is what you do, so you and your wife are not in harmony. She wails in the rental bedroom, the couple who took a picture of the wife eating her husband's ass in the next one over.

The worst part comes when you make comments with your old friend about the backside of a woman in a leather jacket. Soon after that, duck into a bookstore down an alley near Jackson Square, where a comely older woman sits at a chair surrounded by curated books. Fondle a novel, a first edition, and your wife snatches it from your hands.

Something is wrong, you can tell, but you thought everything was great. With friends, or people who used to be, you are far from cheesy colleagues who love Disney cruises.

Be unable to interpret the sadness as the worker rings your wife up with a handwritten paper receipt.

From the novel is the quote, '*I love you and you are lovely.*' You wrote that on a bookmark, gave it to your lady on a barren street under a streetlamp, by a quiet park near a deep cold lake.

You should have included the part right before in the novel, about rendezvous in sand traps and friendly bumping into nurses from behind, about inviting college girls in black leather jackets into the gloaming.

Mostly fight on the trip. Later, try to joke about how all trips you take with your lady are 'fight trips.' Fly home.

Back in the brick apartment, work on your next book, a book of rejected stories. *The editors were only publishing the people they wanted to see naked*, you believe.

A degree in mental health counseling is the next plan. Dive into the process, collecting signatures, transcripts, references. Drive ten hours one day for a group interview on the plains.

A week later, in the brick apartment, primp yourself for a video interview. The women on the screen seem collegial. Imagine, as you listen to their cheery questions, driving from your parents' house to the land grant university two hours away.

A month passes.

The mental health counseling program accepts you. Before deciding what to do, publish a book of short stories. No one buys short stories, you tell yourself, seeing no one has bought even a copy, so why blubber.

Support comes from your wife, who works by day, studies for boards at night, and decides one July night, on the wobbly porch of a duplex in the cheesy suburbs, where you have moved to be closer to her work, you will not go to graduate school on the plains.

The next morning, wife gone to work, masturbate in the shower, to a picture of a woman on your Finsta. She stretches in a thong, becoming like a fleshy pretzel, and her caption says:

You are stronger than they could ever imagine. A warrior. A goddess.

Watch your life wash away again with inconsequential water. Dry off, get dressed, go to your computer on a long wooden table, and be worn out with desire to have someone in your mentions say, 'You're a crazy talented writer, Henry.'

Listen, that evening, and every evening, to your wife tell stories about work, where she is stressed. On the weekends, go on long walks, canvassing the rusted city by the deep cold lake. Add to a journal you will later turn into another novel about how you are worn out with desire, for honor, fame, anything more than the dusty crumbs of nothing you have.

One Saturday, walking through the city without ayahuasca, aliens have not covered your body in obsidian liquid, lubing you for a holy orgy, and you have that book of stories to publish. Your goal on the walk is a used bookstore miles to the south, in Greenfield. Appear as a vagrant to the drivers going past. Not high from cactus juice, you are not floating on a sea of ancestral mushrooms in charge of how grass grows. Sweat seeps through your two pairs of elastic boxer briefs into blue cotton shorts, detailing for the passing drivers your body.

Walk as someone who did not lose your body's virginity to a female extra-terrestrial demon descended from Mother Gia but to a halfsie preschool teacher you met at your job in Sioux Falls, delivering meals to her class. This was before meeting Susannah from Myspace, who spoke with Christ, who told her you were not the one for her after three days inside her room in a mansion.

Before Susannah is Belladonna, the preschool teacher with mocha skin.

By now, inside Harold, you know you are not supposed to describe skin using food, but that's what you do. Belladonna smoked weed. She adorned her bedroom walls with drawings of a tough-looking ex. She first invited you over to watch *Jersey Shore*.

Remember her going to her kitchen for popcorn. Travel through time and follow again. Kneel before her. Look up, at Belladonna's hands against the wall. Next, bent over her couch, she wears socks. Sunlight streams in as Belladonna pounds against you. You have freed yourself of boyhood.

Then is Susannah, then the Christian housebuilders in Cascadia, then the private college graduates in the rented attic. Later, you live along a deep cold lake, and you walk through the cheesy suburbs in the heat of summer, to sweat out the toxins of the past.

You have apostatized. With faith, you think as you walk, Christ may have shined His favor. You might be published by now.

His heat bellows down. Continue your obscure walk.

THE EXTINCTION MANUAL XII

This morning my thoughts
Are as disordered
As my black hair
                    -Lady Horikawa

Summer ends.

Reach out to Claire. She worked first shift at the job in West Allis. Claire had a soft voice, laughed a lilting laugh, and joked around with you. Full-bodied, she grew up Christian but by the time you knew her she lived with a programmer boyfriend. You only ever exchanged flirty texts before she left the cubicle near the fairgrounds and began a new job she said paid more.

'They're hiring,' she texts. 'You should apply.' Claire puts in a good word.

Go to an interview conducted by a thin man who compliments your scattered resume.

'What haven't you done?' he says.

In a cramped room, the thin man goes on about what his company does. Daydream the whole time he talks but affirm yes when he calls later that day with an offer to do whatever it is the job requires. You assume, as with any job, you will figure it out as you go along. Theoretical instructions, as in the thin man's speech about the job in the cramped room, are not engaging by nature.

On your first day, an administrative assistant shows you to your cubicle in a warehouse with lofty ceilings. Once, this was a big box store.

Plopping down the company manual, the administrative assistant's sweat drips on your tabletop. There is a yellow noodle soup stain on your left wall.

'Sorry,' she says, 'hot flashes,' and leaves you to read.

Later that morning, Claire arrives but does not say hello, acting out a scene from your old work near the fairgrounds where everyone was hardened. She comes over at some point, not for long, which makes you think Claire does not want to embarrass herself in front of her new colleagues. A contingent has graduate degrees. The others, with a BS by their name on their business cards, can make up their own schedule. The thin man allows them that. Many use their boss's grace to take home full pay but work part time. You learn the gossip on training visits, riding in speeding social workers' cars, clutching the bottom of their passenger seats.

Hearing those bleak stories on those terrifying rides makes you finally realize you are not a social worker. You are a guy who wants to get paid to yearn in journals he will later call novels about the women with yoga bodies he sees and can never have.

A month of training passes. One afternoon at work, in the fall, in your beaten Malibu outside the warehouse building, eat a crisp apple. Crunch and look up at towering trees, planted long ago. A nice zephyr flows through your car, as you think: *This is how life should be, to have purpose, get paid, and eat healthy.*

In the next second, know you need to go inside. Training is over. You are to become one of the two men at the job. The other, a pot-bellied chain-smoker, laughs hard at his own jokes.

That night in the duplex on the green couch, tell your wife your decision. She agrees. She knows how overburdened social workers are. The next morning go in and tell your three bosses that you and your wife are leaving the state when her fellowship ends.

'It doesn't feel right investing more time,' you tell your three bosses. 'Wouldn't be fair to me, and to you guys.'

You signed no contract. They have no other option than to disapprovingly say, 'Good luck.'

A Masculine Trilemma

Now hand in your badge, to the one who sweat on your dirty cubicle the first day. She accepts it, says good luck. She does not tell you that Claire will not speak to you again.

THE EXTINCTION MANUAL XIII

What pain which is only felt by the body can be compared to this pain?
- Jean Paul

Alone and unemployed, you are more self-published. The giveaways for your latest book amount to sending your 'whole heart' to housewives in rural North Dakota and Alabama. Receive two-star reviews in return.

Do not tell your family. On a visit home to the plains, your wife hardly speaks. She regrets coupling with you, you fear. If alone, you would die alone, like Meline, who perished after too many rants against the people he needed to befriend.

You do not know Important Creative anymore. The private college graduates are in the frozen north. Engendering friendships with them is what you should have been doing, not falling for them, so there would have been no falling out, and one day they could have cordially introduced you to their *cousin in publishing*.

Never should you have told them they were 'cavalier with love.' Too stuck dumb by their fat backsides that caused public scandals, like the plain shopgirls in Meline's world.

Separated from Important Creatives, you are unemployed again after a week at a coffee roaster in rusted city. Before starting there, you entertained hopes of working beside happy young people who played grabass while filling bags of coffee beans. Instead, the job meant you answered to a chubby man about your age with a scraggly beard and a blues rock band on the side. You told him, one afternoon early on, that you didn't appreciate him telling you, after he had done so more than once, to 'get over here.' Shocked at the insubordination, the scraggly, chubby man tattled to your peaceful second boss, and you got the heave-ho.

A Masculine Trilemma

'It was beneath you,' your wife consoles you that night in the crumbling duplex, though you fear you are devolving, like a character from a bad drug novel who one day finds himself in back alleys, exchanging services.

There could be art school, you begin to think, and in working toward a degree in creative writing you could bide your time. In a couple years, the world will have descended into civil war, and after the destruction there will be only a few caring about the distinction between 'regular' and 'self-published.'

THE EXTINCTION MANUAL XIV

Stop fearing "art for art's sake" as the worst of evils
- Robbe-Grillet

Now in the present, inside a study room in Harold, graduate school in the arts coming to an end, with no more hope than when you started, you are without the courage to fly into a river after years of fresh undergraduates with round assess telling you your words were the first they fell in love with in high school that encouraged them to write their own stories which they read to you in their dorm room. Posters of vintage movies, smell of weed in the air, and when she finishes her story, she looks up at you timidly.

'It's great,' you say, assuring her. As a man of distinction, of letters, you can assure her easily. She asks once more, that's all.

'Really?' She asks, as a junior.

'Yes,' you say, and she lowers her sweet head. You are thankful for her efforts.

You do not have that. You have not fallen into a frozen river after readings where you were considered reclusive but honoring those serious regarding the pursuit of writing about their troubles in not finding enough or finding too much.

No Distinguished Journal has swept you off your feet with a direct message, asking if they could whisk your books to the editing factory for a scrubbing behind the ears so they can come out shiny, with new coordinated covers, like the plain ones they use in Paris.

Sit in that library study room, just done reading a tweet about how you should just 'go away from literature altogether.' Sit there, wishing for the life of someone who goes on late night television and has observations on *the state of America's ontological crisis*. Wish, daydream, look at your phone, at a repeating triptych called a *titty drop*. It brings the pain of longing.

A Masculine Trilemma

Five or five hundred more will not make you known, but there was no helping it, so you did this, which began with writing about fifty of your favorite novels. You abandoned that when you thought of how doing that would only be rejected, so you did this, thinking another would not make you as sad, though it has made you sadder, after years of shaping for no one.

II

BEFORE A LONG WOODEN TABLE

A Masculine Trilemma

If I had to do it all over again,
I wouldn't
-Berryman

BEFORE A LONG WOODEN TABLE I

Being more concerned for their husband's reputation than for anything else, they take care and trouble to have as many fellow-wives as possible, since that is a testimony to their husband's valor.

-Montaigne

I should be honest.

On another morning before going to work in a cubicle near the fairgrounds in West Allis I spent an hour in this crumbling duplex in the cheesy suburbs searching for a video I saw once, of a female folk group, harmonizing in a forest. I saw them, once, those hippies in the woods, banging on guitar cases. They were thick nymphets, singing in harmony. I could not find their song, full-figured and illusive, like Three Graces, and now their memory is like trying to make a fist in a dream but being unable.

Knowing I wasted an hour searching for those sirens explains why I am in the cheesy suburbs and not in a Brooklyn loft, being paid well to say how people born like me should die in a fire.

Christ, I know as a husband before a long wooden table, I should not criticize the Important Creatives, not when I have fallen for fair poets with curly auburn hair in only wire glasses. I squandered days mourning those private college graduates in a colder, less relevant Brooklyn, called Minneapolis.

Now all I know is shame, remembering a time, in Cascadia, when I had a chance to make but could not stop drinking cheap wine and worshiping housebuilder forms. I made nothing then, like now in this crumbling duplex.

My only consolation is perfect art exists: *Submission, Milo and Otis,* the ba ba ba ba ba basketball skit. May as well spend hours searching for clear-eyed songstresses humming in sarongs.

A Masculine Trilemma

More inane thoughts assail me, like how this morning on social media I supported a dissenting woman. She disagreed with an Important Creative who said the hijab is a 'symbol of empowerment.'

Never should I be critical of religion.

Under a theocracy, I know before this long wooden table, I could have wives, and instead of Amateur Mansplainer I could have the title of Important Creative. Only commenting on state-sanctioned topics, I know, but I would not care about my muzzle as my youngest wife with subtle breasts and a wild bush and large backside brings me grapes to nibble, as to give me a break from writing my *portraits of real life*.

A Finsta will help, I really think now, and social media will be what sells my novels, *then* I will no longer need to go to a cubicle near the fairgrounds, and athletic women smelling of fruity shampoos will visit the airy office I use for composing Important Fiction, and they will come in opening their new jackets from Madewell. After I give them a reviving, they will know to leave (with hope to see me again), as to allow me to 'get some work done.'

BEFORE A LONG WOODEN TABLE II

I thought I was wounded to the core
but I was only bruised
-Levertov

Now from before this long wooden table, as I listen through
headphones to a German man spin dance music at a chill party in Tulum, I
pluck forearm hairs twined with glue from a temporary tat, and, I think, unless
a Samoan, or a sailor in the 1940s, no one should have permanent markings.

Lord, I know, I should be more forgiving.

We want to attract the beefiest mate. Designs and colors lure her.
Like a bird of paradise has plumage, we want to hypnotize athletic females, by
wearing woodsy colognes, diamond watches, rolled-up jeans. Symbols denote
status to attain a better-paying job, so a man can afford a lavish cave, to entice
a well-built female to want to build a nest for us so cozy no other females
could ever be fresh enough for their man to want to mount.

A personal ethology I put down before going to the cubicle near the
fairgrounds, when I should be drafting a poem, using descriptions like *hefty
stars*, and *mossy trees*. I should think of how to employ *milky* as an adjective.
I should name a flower.

I just cannot think. My blood sugar drops. My limbs become tingly.
A current pulsates through my blood, so I went to the kitchen. Facing another
duplex, I ate cold noodles.

Levels refilled, now back at the long wooden table, my social media
numbers are still meager. The best I can hope for, if everything goes right
from this second to the moment I die, I am mentioned in an episode of a teen
drama in a high-speed conversation about dead authors, and I should be glad
for that. I should be glad I have never been inside the shadow of a fallen

waxwing too. That would be a terrifying passerine I hope I never see, or I do hope to, near the end and wishing for birds the size of airplanes and caterpillars the size of Caterpillars.

This morning, I should add, before going to slump into the grey cloth today, I came across an Australian who invites friends to her studio and they undress, massage yonis, reach acmes. After each session, as I imagined before this long wooden table, the studio must be rank from the raw material of exerting bodies.

Based on her social media photos, the instructor has her choice between a silver fox and a lean young buck, hair slicked back into a bun. The instructor's aura reminded me of another, a yoga teacher who announced every one of her privileged choices from Minneapolis to Brooklyn and back again. I fell for her without meeting. I wanted her, even after she spent a good chunk of our two-hour phone conversation talking to me about an alcoholic ex. He lived on a farm in Wisconsin, she told me, and I never interrupted from my rented attic with, 'Your alcoholic ex isn't so special.' Because, I know, she would have been so offended. She wanted, wants still, I am sure, now in Wisconsin, everything she saw or touched to be *the most special thing*. Her bread and salt, to know it was the *most amazing*, what she heard, tasted, or felt.

I wanted to be one of her meaningful nuggets then. I worked at a corporate bookstore, lived in a rented attic, and slept on a mattress on the floor. Before moving to those frozen suburbs of Minneapolis I grew up on the plains, without ever driving a combine.

In that rented attic, I remember I thought after that yoga teacher went silent, if I had driven a combine, my life's orbit would have tilted, and I would have seemed manly and not yearned so much for a yoga teacher slash copywriter who lived *intentionally* in Minneapolis and Brooklyn, and she would not have sensed my desperation and cancelled our plans twice and before we were to at last meet for coffee she would not have sent her last text:

'On second thought I don't want to meet you, so good luck w/ whatever you're looking for.'

Now on her website I see she offers guided meditations, along with a love note if you follow her newsletter. She must be back with her alcoholic ex, I think before this long wooden table. There is a picture of her with a dead-eyed man, and the caption reads: 'We look cute sometimes.' That update makes me want to weep.

For her, yes, but also for someone who thought if he had driven a combine in youth he might not have, as a man, received a curt goodbye from a stranger and years later commented on the past through a journal he calls a novel, thinking he had found some pathetic balancing of the ledger.

BEFORE A LONG WOODEN TABLE III

And my heart is as heavy as
A Damascan woman's ass
-Apollinaire

There is hunger to sate, the cubicle to go to, Christian girlfriends to reminisce about. Worse, I do not care about Christian girlfriends, which is not true. I care of immortalizing Christian girlfriends as I care to be an Important Creative in Brooklyn paid to tweet about how 'the former Cheeto-in-chief is still colluding with the Russians tbh.'

Really, I believe, it would be great to be close with the Russians after they have twerked and showered. Brown from tanning under the Caucasian sun, white-robed, they would speak to me with a warm tongue into my naked ear:

'Brother coming to steal money, chop body, put parts in icy river.'

And I would not care. All would be right with the world with my Russian fitness influencer.

Tomorrow, more of this, more worshipping yoga women and athletic influencers, more asking the gods why I cannot remember the difference between trenchant and truculent, more vacillating on searching the latest by Abella.

If someone like her visited my mattress in the frozen suburbs, she would have blessed me. The following day, I imagine before this long wooden table, pregnant with waiting, and when her terse text came it would have been about how great I am, but things are *sooo busy rn*. Weeks of replaying everything then, of concentrating on the intimate moments, sure she went on to find someone unable to fit inside her.

Instead of online dating in frozen suburbs, I know now, I should have researched the sounds coming from Saturn's rings. I would not have uncovered any knowledge of cosmogony, but at least I would not have pestered anyone about falling in love.

How much better it would have been to avoid texts about why everything is so busy.

And still I wonder of Abella.

How powerful it would be, to at any moment cause thousands to lose the substance that could give life.

What I mean, back from the shower, is I do not understand what I do, as Paul did not, when he wrote to the Romans.

Before a long wooden table, I think of my decaying life before driving to the cubicle in West Allis. If I did what I wanted to do I would be massaging the big asses of yoga women in Tulum. I have as much control over what I do as my heart does in beating.

A better theological argument could be argued for what the devotees of submission desire: *Less culture, more breeding.* For those scriptures I would shout in the streets: 'There is too much profanity in women, and not enough polyamory, for men.'

I blaspheme before a long wooden table when I should be going online, engaging with young singles about a recently published literary fiction story, how it is 'about dismantling white supremacy and the patriarchy tbh.' I should tweet, 'We must all be *so* tender,' and elicit a great many 'yes this,' but I keep thinking about the sparkling soda to my right, and why? For using a question mark, Gertrude would say I am trash.

As this trash, I was born past the time when my kind could publish debased fantasies about undergraduate females. The last safe space is fantasy for my kind, and I too want to be paid to think of castles like Gwendorm, for swords like Windblade, maidens like Mona with soft hips. I just cannot. I would stop before finishing a page, stuck in the banality: the only reason we need new stories is so they shoot light as we drink wine in our rented room, and hear our online date ask, 'Do you give head rubs?'

'You haven't heard?' you reply, beside her on your prized black pleather couch. 'I give the best head rubs.'

The fantasy story plays, wine warms, and now you are married with two children, worrying about the cleanliness of your gutters in Eden Prairie.

Incremental increases in the temperature of a relationship worked into a slow boil, cooking you away from an honest, single life. She never wanted you with others, though the both of you knew you still would want the exhilaration of a new body, yet with each choice, going out again with your online date instead of staying home, a weekend getaway with her, meeting the parents, buying a ring, inviting cousins you haven't seen in years to a church you haven't gone to in longer, you locked in after watching a fantasy show on cable.

The way to avoid all that is by stripping desire. No longer ask pretty waitresses into the gloaming. Before this long wooden table, I know I would never be able to shed the impulses of coveting, of burning. I want more as I want more excreting.

Soon for me is a cubicle near the fairgrounds where everyone will be slumping. Cockroaches on the bathroom floor there, burnt popcorn in the microwave. If choice existed, I would not go, but choice is a fairy tale, like with Mona, the busty maid, and Clawsteel, the legendary sword.

After enough of this, we are told in scriptures, we walk to the light to be with the creator of the universe who will provide us virgins for eternity.

A way to distract from the wanting is to go online and preach to strangers about what is debased and what is holy. The dialogue enriching technocrats helps, we tell ourselves.

The answer is not more novels, as those are bricks meant to woo big-assed undergraduates with an interest in publishing their own stories. Everyone would be better off putting their heads in ovens.

And still I listen through headphones to a mix spun by a German in Tulum and dream of shoulder swaying with the privileged spring breakers: the one with long dark curls, the relaxed blonde, and the one in a diaphanous white blouse who flips her hair to one side.

I am not nodding my head with them in Mexico. I am about to go to a cubicle near the fairgrounds. I should lie in a muddy ditch. I should eat the dead grass.

BEFORE A LONG WOODEN TABLE IV

To whatever degree he may have desacralized the world, the man who has made his choice in favor of a profane life never succeeds in completely doing away with religious behavior.
- *Eliade*

A long walk to a poetry bookstore in Riverwest, I could not muster it.

My plan: take pictures along the way. As if, I say now before a long wooden table, as if photographing the deterioration of a city would have gotten me noticed by those in charge of noticing. I did not want to sweat gross man fat, in the poetry bookstore buy nothing, and leave millions of thoughts produced from billions of hours spent alone. Instead of going I stayed in the crumbling duplex with my wife. On the green couch, as she shopped on her device, I read:

'The whole world can be divided into those who write and those who do not. Those who write represent despair, while those who read disapprove of despair and believe they have a superior wisdom, and yet, if they were able to write, they would write the same thing.'

A walk, or writing, neither could I bear taking up my Sunday. Thumbing through the ambitions of sociopaths who call themselves poets held no appeal. Worse, as a husband, no motivation. No point in meeting eyes with her in an empty aisle. I look down to see her copy of *Lady Fantasies,* and she sees my copy of *Man Feelings*. With hair on my back I am dreading the cubicle, here without the strength to support the industry that could sustain my imaginary dream future. Instead of the poetry bookstore, I came upon the epiphany for a novel. My wife on the green couch, scrolling on her device, I wrote in my phone: 'Everyone dies in the first sentence.'

Later, walking back to the crumbling duplex after mounting the courage to go to a suburban library to pick up books (Elaide, Guénon, Nolte),

I thought of a standup routine starting with a bit about being on a sidewalk and someone on their phone is coming toward you and you know they will walk into you if you don't take evasive action.

Now near the time to go to the cubicle on a Monday, I wonder, did the enjoyment of the joke hinge on the presentation? Before a long wooden table, nothing is funny, and I am realizing, even if I were published by the Important Creatives, I would bog the world down, so it is *good* to be this disappointed. At a certain level of not having, it is impossible to keep trying.

Quickly I remember when I announced the release of my novel about online dating. Only Stacy replied. Instead of congratulations, she replied to say she was engaged.

Stacy wanted to tell me that for so long, I know now before a long wooden table, ever since we lived down the street from each other in McKennan Park. Stacy still lived in Sioux Falls when I, later in the frozen suburbs of Minneapolis, sent her a link to my blog, with its thoughts on literature and reposted photos of full-bodied millennials in well-lit city apartments from a softcore website catering to guys who had seen a Bergman film or two. Stacy never replied to my email about my blog that I thought at the time would be my ticket to being known.

From her silence I understood Stacy pitied me. I had given into to hedonism and was going to hell. Not until years later, after a bald bearded man slid a ring on Stacy's finger, did she have her power.

Still, I was glad when Stacy responded to my tweet. She filled the empty space. The algorithm never pushed my updates to Important Creatives. Even if it had, I know before this long wooden table they would have thought, 'It's only self-published,' and felt the same embarrassment Stacy felt when she saw my personal blog, with its pictures of subtly tattooed women on sunlit beds. Too intimate, the Important Creatives would have looked away. Unlike

Stacy, who used my announcement as a sounding board to exclaim her victory of the blessings from Christ.

And still Stacey made me less lonely. When I saw her notification, I remember now from before a long wooden table, for a second, I did not wallow in the silence of my supposed accomplishment.

Years ago, all that, back when I first moved to this rusted city by the deep cold lake. Now I am tired, about to go to a cubicle near the fairgrounds after thinking of but not writing about Christian girlfriends, like Susannah, who works in a loft in Oxford now, I see through my Finsta. She arranges products for commercials.

If Susannah still believes, only God knows. All I know is Susannah no longer posts inspirational scriptures. No mention of Christ after her sister has a baby. A backslide? Maybe. Maybe Susannah is now without a husband who leads their non-denominational church, though I doubt it.

The week I went to see Susannah, I suffered from an outbreak of acne. I lived in Sioux Falls then, down the street from Stacey, and my face was one thing Susannah would fix. After I went to see her, she sent me a neti pot, to eradicate the dark circles under my eyes, and she would become a sculptor too, she told me in her room in a mansion. Now I am self-published four times over, while Susannah has become a manager for products. A perverse part of me wants to follow her, but my body will not allow it, knowing how Susannah will see the notification and look at the bikini fitness influencers I like, the depressing number of hearts on my posts, my paltry follower count.

So, I do nothing in the quiet before work, and as the seconds tick by the awful heaviness of dread increases.

BEFORE A LONG WOODEN TABLE V

And I am seized with long-unwonted yearning
Toward yonder realm of spirits grave and still.
-Goethe

I cringe from before this long wooden table, thinking how I gave away my vanity to a coworker. Soon after was a tap on my shoulder, shocking me with static electricity. A different coworker, whom I know less, stood in my cubicle, right on my plastic mat.

'Disappointed in you,' she said, wagging her finger, close enough I smelled her orange perfume.

'Oh?' I said, playing dumb.

'You didn't tell me you were a *published author.*'

And she pulled out my first self-published book from behind her back, had me sign it and told me the other coworker said it was fine, that I could give them a different copy.

Now, in these curdled suburbs, I know foreign armies made of anime characters march in synchronicity. Maybe, I think before this long wooden table, if I could be a Japanese teen inside of a Pikachu costume, I might wave a stubby arm with tourists, but I am not in a Pikachu costume, nor am I planning trips with former Christian friends.

A reassurance comes in this sameness of monogamy which abuts the dread of monotony. Gerrymandering might occur if I just decide, like a man, to just get on a plane and go to a cabin at the foot of the Cascades.

My wife would never permit it. She hates the saved ones I slipped in and out of bed with in young manhood, those Christian women who like to brag about the guys they have been with since. Emotions don't get the best of them.

'...not like they do with your wife,' one red-haired one named Hannah told me in secret over chat.

Before a long wooden table I am filled with knowing there are trips of Christian grabass I will never take. Never will I see vast portions of this world, only the same stretches of miserable interstate taking me to a cubicle near the fairgrounds and home again to a crumbling duplex. I could prank former Christian friends, say I *will* be coming to the reunion, but they will only think I am being cruel. Nothing like in youth when everything was a joke or a prelude to a kiss. Everything now is a regret, and that I argue internally makes me think I have a chance, like I am tabulating the best uses of my time to allow maximum space for *the act of creation.*

All the while my phone receives updates. And that upgrading makes me believe I am improving, that I am growing large. The idea of increasing makes me think of last night, when a full-bushed Indian, Kali, who in the dream said she was a 'sophomore majoring in dance at a private college,' swam in an indoor pool. None of the signs, tied to floating balloons, forbid making out, so I asked to talk with a manager, who was my 6th grade teacher, and they had no recourse. None of the signs restricted 'hanky-panky,' as I said in the dream.

Before the Indian and I entered the water, I was naked, titling back my head with confidence in a place that was like a set for a play.

Now that dream is recorded and my former landlord in the frozen suburbs would be so bored. He hated the retelling of what he believed amounted to the 'excrement of our subconscious.' We met proselytizing in Colorado before I moved to Cascadia, where I waxed yachts by day and at night went to bed with postmodern Christians who had moved to the Pacific Northwest to help the poor. The one I must have loved, Greer, went to Bellingham for college. The next years I spent bemoaning my inaction while becoming balder, and now in this crumbling duplex we need groceries. My wife will soon despair. I wait for her text:

We need groceries. God, I hate that we don't have any.

Christ, please throw a spear, hard at me before a long wooden table, or make me get online and engage with every Important Creative. Instead this morning I ate bean burritos, washed the dishes, and before her work I bumbled to my wife about the elections.

'A sociologist said the media propped up the centrist candidate,' I said as I ate an Eggo on the green couch.

'You know, so the richies can keep everything status quo for their lives where they go on vacation every August and give platitudes about the terrors of racism while drinking the finest natural wines.'

'They're ready for a new culture to take their place,' I said after her silence. 'They believe they deserve to be erased.'

Dismayed, I think by the life she chose with me, my wife picked up her undrank coffee, got up from the green couch, and left for work.

BEFORE A LONG WOODEN TABLE VI

Nothing leads a man astray so easily as sexual desire. What a foolish thing a man's heart is!
-Kenko

Unity, always tan, curly haired, drove from her parents' place in Eden Prairie. To me in Nordeast, where we played video games in my upper level. Unity only stopped talking when she knelled. After she finished me, I would watch her walk to the shower like a peeping tom. Her backside was so impressive, I remember I once thought, watching her go, 'That must start discussions among couples behind her.'

Poor but happy, enjoying threesomes in Minneapolis, would have been us, but I left her for this place along a deep cold lake. After I did, Unity sent me naked pictures of the women she chose through her phone with her next 'Dom,' as she called him, college girls with unformed frontal lobes, full faces, wide eyes.

If only Unity would now walk through the door of this crumbling duplex, skirt loose around her thighs, snug around her waist, tell me how it was hard for her to find clothes that fit, flip up that skirt, push me against her warmth, so it is like I am underneath one of those tarps in elementary school at gym class, as in that position I would not worry about bearded men in Brooklyn whose banality has been published in many languages or my wife's Polish friend who is seeing a lawyer who, according to her Polish friend, 'does not need to plan dates.'

'He just shows up at my place,' my wife's Polish friend said.

Related, I was remiss in removing my back hair over the weekend. Usually my wife helps, spreading a cream, curling the hair, and scraping me with a plastic spatula. Related because I am sure that the Polish friend's man is hairless, except for patches under his arms and balls. I mean to say I am

71

wanting, like the Important Creatives tweeting that a woman fighting for the rights of women to not wear what men prescribe is the 'wrong feminist for these times.'

So many people want so many things, and all I want is for Unity to walk up the stairs of this crumbling duplex with straight hair, carrying a Tupperware of dried flowers, and for her to say, 'Tried something different with it...do you like it?'

Christ, I know I would die an agonizing death if my wife ever found this. Still private, I could add, this weekend, the plan is to meet Kaliyah from first shift and give her my books. Kaliyah left the bad job I still work for another. Her lilting laugh made our stale office warm and now I wonder what it would have been like if we had met before all this misery. For months, good times, later, as I imagine before this long wooden table, an amicable split, and now I would have memories of the way Kaliyah reverberated.

BEFORE A LONG WOODEN TABLE VII

The sexual organs are the true seat of the will, of which the opposite pole is the brain
- Schopenhauer

How shameful, that for our meeting I picked an outfit and walked all groomed, smelling like soap. Like a waxed car, rain dripped off me in beads, and there in the bar's parking lot Kaliyah and I embraced. She noticed my unzipped fly. I think I had accidently not zipped. I think. Sitting across from her in a booth I tried to interpret her body language and I wondered if she thought I looked different than my profile, though we had known each other at a terrible job.

Now before this long wooden table I deserve to grimace, to wince, to think of once upon a time, in the frozen suburbs, when I quit my job at a corporate bookstore so I could focus on writing a novel about online dating. All the while I submitted to culture magazines like *Feeling Magazine* and *Sin*. I failed to find a foothold in that Important Creative world, so I moved to a duplex in Nordeast, took a full-time job at a steelyard. A good while later, I think before a long wooden table, if I could just get out of this crumbling duplex, walk east, join up with artists in Riverwest, I might find someone who would publish me, feature me in Woodland Pattern, and I am asked to join the radio show with Mark from *American Movie*, where we talk about the struggle to be an artist, and someone on NPR hears, and from there is the shiny life of an Important Creative in Brooklyn.

Even in dreams, I sell out. Mark from the American movie made a way for himself in this rusted city. Never did he move to a gilded playground like Williamsburg or Madison, places where they have marches for people *of color* but where no one *of color* lives.

73

Christ, I kept my wedding ring in a drawer at home and Kaliyah wore lipstick. Nails painted deep red, Kaliyah noticed my fly unzipped after she emerged from her van in the parking lot of the dive bar in the cheesy suburbs. Now, alone in the crumbling duplex, I am sure Kaliyah drove into a ditch after she drank a vodka tonic and two beers. The police will come talk with me, the last man who saw my former coworker, and I will have to explain what we drank and ate, beers and poutine, given to us by a fresh-faced waitress who was sensitive and pure and who I loved, so my wife, away at work on the weekend, will know I met with a woman and that woman wore lipstick, drank three drinks, and drove away.

Kaliyah has not texted me. Authorities at the door of this crumbling duplex, I will be outed: as a worm who keeps his wedding ring at home when he goes for drinks with meaty former coworkers.

Christ, I got back to the crumbling duplex and ate leftover fried shrimp. I cannot stop, is what I mean, this eating, wanting.

BEFORE A LONG WOODEN TABLE VIII

> For man's greatest offence
> Is that he has been born
> *-Calderón*

Never thought I would become A Neutered Man, That Husband Guy, cut off from old female friends by order of his wife. No longer am I allowed to 'stay in touch.' Either endure fights for defending my choices as someone who kept speaking with those who once texted me their self-reddened asses, or acquiesce to the rightful assertions I am, as my wife once told me, 'without a frontal lobe.'

Again without, I remember before this long wooden table, a former self after college, religious and single in Sioux Falls, and everyone had college girlfriends turning into wives. Not so unusual where I came from. I stood up as a groomsman at 19, for the wedding of a classmate, and here I am without children (that classmate has six) wanting to be someone who makes Charley or Fette jealous. Charley, I knew before she was awarded best YA novelist in Minnesota. Heavier now, not as athletic big, more just big, Charley's girth makes me want her more.

Pointless to think of Fette too. She teaches creative writing at St. Goethe now but once messaged me her number, asked for a drink. We exchanged stories, like a game of 'I'll show you mine if you show me yours,' then I went silent, fearing being caught by my girlfriend now wife. Now those women are what I want to be, called important by people who tweet links to reviews of obscure novels. Worse now, before this long wooden table, to think of Adriana. I looked her up to jump-start this nameless day. At pho against The Greenway Adriana asked me my favorite novels. She brought along a journal and pen and dutifully recorded what I said. Weeks later, Adriana texted that I 'yearned too much.'

Married now, in her social media profile Adriana wears a black leather dress a psychotherapist would say communicates bound desires and here I am writing my wastebooks that could never inspire jealousy, not with Adriana and her Important Creative friends. Over pho against The Greenway, Adriana told me she planned to set her debut novel in China. She said 'debut novel' as if she knew it to be a foregone conclusion, that one day someone would publish her and she would release this statement:

'Guys, some personal news. My novel is coming out with Known Creative Press in 2056.'

A novel's release must be set far into the future, Important Creatives believe, when all a novel needs is private college interns with waxed crotches and hairy armpits working until there are no errors, then an avalanche of money to bully the public into reading.

Now, alone in this crumbling duplex, I want Adriana to be pained that she chose the chubby bearded man I see on her social feed and not me. This would not make her hurt. This would give her joy, this journal proving I am a desperate yearner never published, so I am not a real man.

This weekend I will make it worse, walking to a used bookstore in this rusted city, browsing through shelves representing millions of hours spent alone, and I will think on the walk: I have massaged and finished on the asses of private college graduates, yes, but it is the asses I have not massaged and finished upon I fantasize about, wondering, if I ever got published by Known Creative Press, a new crop of private college graduates might want me. I will go on this long walk so the most athletic ones would want to read my words and drench their twin bed in desire.

The wanting is like a fire, so I just went online and found a poet in San Francisco, with a groomed mound, small tits and a manly yet beautiful face. Watching her read her poetry has not made me known. Neither does an Italian named Valentina, taking down her cozy pajamas, sitting on an average man until he disappears. Keep going, I could, but no matter how long I do I will never find one of the private college graduates I knew for a month in the frozen suburbs before they left for a guy who grew mushrooms and had a book of essays coming out in 2066.

Before this long wooden table, I think of the act of creation instead, how a last work is best. Nearing blackness, the striving is less. That observation does not draw me closer to becoming known, and now before going to the cubicle I admire the tantric yoga teacher named Janabi. When she takes off her sports bra, she reverberates like godly jelly. She will not help me become known. Neither will Jada, cooking in the nude. No matter how earnest Jada's backside or refreshing her strip of bush, I will not get farther. Watching chocolate syrup drizzle over waiting nipples will not help, nor will a modern woman dancing in spandex shorts. Amazing as her wedgie may be, she will not get me closer.

Diversions over, shower over, I can say, after we left a restaurant in Bayview last weekend, after my wife recalled an old boyfriend with a member 'about the size of a soda can,' I came upon a thought that I should tweet: 'Just a short walk on cozy back streets, and it is dusk, and love is starting, and she is so pretty she could make gods weep.'

Christ, if only I had breasts like tangy dollops of meringue, I would not worry about the cringe of tweeting again. A man would make sure things were taken care of. I should die, or go to graduate school and say, 'I'm busy,' and people might believe me. I could pretend I am a special boy, and by the end of those graduate school years the cult of identity will have taken over and all undesirables will need to be exterminated.

I thought that this morning before going to the cubicle and I watched Janabi in her loft. I did my foreign language lesson and mispronounced ancient words, got tired, and searched: 'Curly-haired women with thick thighs.' They made their crescendos, and I have smeared away life from the wood floor. Now I am bored, with the interminable cycle of regeneration, excitement, desire, refractory period, regeneration. If only I once had made a Tumblr that turned into a coffee table book, but my posts, a group of big-boned women, a picture I took of a Polish bar in Riverwest, a quote about suicide, would have been a book called *The Mind of a Straight White Male*. Worse, all morning long I have gone between my email, where for years I have not received a word other than from my wife, and the kitchen, where I paced while eating string cheese dipped in Nutella, before I sat before this long wooden table and believed for a second my work might not be so bad. Dear God, I really thought, 'Maybe something good will happen.'

That is how deranged I have become. My mind has become deformed, so badly I want Audrina to Alena to Ariel in Minneapolis to see me with famous literature friends in the front row of Twins game and regret their chubby bearded husband who works as an adjunct.

'Go hard or go home', Earl raps in these headphones, and I think he is saying I should sell my used Malibu and buy reviews of my books of vanity, or be like Carver, unchosen, mopping floors overnight, hampered by alcohol, never finishing a graduate degree at Iowa, then accidentally meeting the most famous editor of this century.

To be sated from the wanting, I would need that degree from Iowa and a wife who immolates herself to make sure her partner reaches her dreams then to meet the most famous editor in a century, or be as prolific as Jack and chronicle men in the wild, but I was not a child laborer and a teenage oyster pirate. A Nintendo player at nine, a teenage Christian, a psychology major at a land-grant university on the plains devoted to finding The One. That trajectory led me to believe my thoughts can cause my body to shrink.

A Masculine Trilemma

Like in my dream last night, in the house on the plains, I lay with Kaliyah, who morphed into a sports commentator slash Spanish beach handball player. The chimera touched me, and a French blue-haired actress became a grown version of my first girlfriend. In sheer black tights she sat on my lap and started to grind. I woke to the sound of garbage trucks barreling down the cheesy street. No, I did not choose that ending, nor how I was born. Not the famous daughter of Manhattan sculptors, people do not inhale the special thoughts I send into the world.

Walking ten miles this weekend will not help. The plan, after the walk, is to go out for beef brisket, ribs with the fat still attached, pulled pork and sausage links, sides of baked beans, macaroni and cheese, pickles, and wash it all down with ice cold beers. The calories will negate my hours of exercise, and I will reappear from the wilderness, saddled with desire. My obscure wake will ebb into the pavement.

BEFORE A LONG WOODEN TABLE IX

Behind every crazy woman is a man sitting very quietly, saying, 'What? I'm not doing anything.'
-Sharma

No one to talk to about all this, other than my wife, who I cannot talk to about all this. I could wedge these thoughts into a novel about balding I publish myself, which would be only a fraction as good as published by an Important Creative. One, I see in her social media, complains about the size of the man she beds. Maybe, if I wrote as a real man would, that Important Creative would notice me. If my submission to her started like this...

'The butcher lay paper on the wood table. The meat was red and bleeding. My alcoholic wife told me it looked like wine. I agreed and told the butcher to cut us two sirloin strips. We were celebrating. I had won the National Book Award...'

To be noticed, I would need to live with another woman who was not my wife and smoke weed instead of drink and call myself sober and my children baleful. Christ, it is all useless. The wanting continues, like last night in my dream where Kaliyah wore a halter top and loose sweatpants. She pushed her top up, her bottoms down, a black thong beneath. Upon waking, my wife at work, I wanted to text Kaliyah. Even now from before this long wooden table I toy with the idea. These lusts make me sound like I joke, yet I am serious when I say in these cheesy suburbs my wife does not have time to stretch all day in yoga pants. Only Hannah, the red-headed Christian in Cascadia, could I graze and make convulse, so I deleted that draft of a text to Kaliyah and scrolled through curated videos.

One began with a well-formed one bent over before another woman, strapped and pumping, and the one bent-over shaking, saying, 'Oh gosh, I'm coming,' as Hannah would do in Cascadia, and, I wondered, while taking a shower in the cramped bathroom of this crumbling duplex, if that well-formed one censored because she believed in Christ, as Hannah did.

Now dressed and ready for the cubicle, there is regret, wondering if that text to Kaliyah could have been the one that started an exchange ending with her meaty thighs dominating my phone.

Earlier this morning, from before this long wooden table, after my Italian lesson seeped out of my head, I watched Valentina walloping against a lucky unknown. She looked back, a man focused the camera, and Valentina said, 'You like my big butt...cheeks.' I then clicked away and researched what it might be like to live in Sioux Falls, got distracted, and read the synopsis of a hot new novel with a bright cover.

Soon for me is a cubicle, and I am not helping, yet I continue and think about food, of taking nude selfies. Chained to this hard chair, I find myself mad at myself. Not for the chaining, I mean, for the knowing, that I am thinking of spending $40 to enter in a short story contest, so I can receive an email months from now that starts:

'Thank you for your submission but...'

No wonder my wife bewails her condition, married to a man unable to give her a life in a three-bedroom loft somewhere nice, in a coastal city. The best thing that could happen for me is I walk through the Northside of this curdled city and am hung by young Black boys, a race war starts, everything becomes ashes.

'How bleak,' as my wife says.

Christ, I know she should have married a man who gave her the luxury to never work and I should have married someone in love with squats and threesomes. I sit here before a long wooden table and wonder if Jenny and Johnny stayed together, or if Jenny found another slacker guy who plays guitar, drinks PBR, and has those skinny arms but protruding gut kind of body. My country look would not matter, if I made good money. Hot leftie women do not care about the environment, if their man's work contributing to nature's downfall earns well. They want a man who has a nice place which could, in theory, if not in practice, entice a 21-year-old CrossFit coach, but all I do in these cheesy suburbs is go online to see that the poetry of Celan was given one star, and the likes for the review are by Azarakhsh, Barbod, and Zohreh.

A century ago, I imagine before a long wooden table, the townsfolk would have passed off my rants as crazy old man talk. I might have lost a limb in a war, avoided death by consumption, worm fit, ship fever, or horrors. Vanquishing those diseases would have made me a legend, so my teen wife and our four children would have known my genes to be strong, and my land to be fertile. Now I think of Malkova, confident as my old twenty-something wife, and wonder what my agrarian neighbors would have thought of her on the farm in her full-makeup and sheer tights, her backside outlined. The other menfolk pulling the plow, as their donkey died of gout, would have been impressed to the point of heart failure.

Never can I tell my parents all I desire is to write these debased thoughts for a living. Never can I tell my wife of the threesome dream, so from before this long wooden table I emailed an Important Creative in Brooklyn about both, asking her to review my novels. She has not responded, will never, and I understand. I did not graduate from a private college where they produce connected Important Creatives. I do not have an agent friend in Greenpoint who promises to publish my debut about growing up in Florida where everything is *hilariously dark* but also *very deep intellectually*. That Important Creative's silence reminds me of the Arab reviewers of Celan. They must assert themselves, or their old rivals will say they do not exist.

'Stay positive,' my wife says, yet I cannot, not when a cubicle waits, and tonight, after returning to the crumbling duplex, I will complain to her on the green couch that I am not what I want to be while I stay what I am, but I will not tell her what I am, as she already knows she married a lusting idiot who thinks of Malkova's thick thighs squeezing him until his brains are squished on the sidewalk, like the fruit of a watermelon.

BEFORE A LONG WOODEN TABLE X

My passion for round, warm, dark Jewish girls was insatiable
                                                    -Kentfield

Now before leaving this crumbling duplex for another afternoon and evening in the cubicle, I think of Van Gogh at Saint Remy, where he said, 'I cannot describe what I have…the empty fatigue and vague melancholy, the atrocious remorse.'

Sectioned to this hard chair I bemoan my lot of not having a job where I teach the art of authoring made-up stories to private college students formed in the ideal bean shape, as Crumb described. Everyone I know is relieved I have this sentence, glad I have work at the cubicle and do not just 'do nothing.' I do nothing. I go to a country singer's social media and admire her in a one-piece American flag bathing suit. I watch Perry jumping into a crowd of believers in the Illinois cornfields. As a teen, I see from before a long wooden table, Perry was grown, already gaining the kind of attention that would lead her away from heaven and into piles of money. From before a long wooden table I desire to be a pansexual Muslim with an arts degree from a private college and a creative writing degree from the Workshop.

Ranting will not help, nor will searching for Bill's old ladies, Joanna and Chan, who must have loved Bill's boyish graying hair and songs about love and eagles. My own inventory, remembering Cassandra. At a bar in St. Paul, we drank local beers. A day later, in my rented attic, I visited her Tumblr, hoping to find evidence of her excitement, only to find a post about an interaction with her grandmother.

'It's okay, Cassandra. You just must wait until you meet someone who gives you stomach bubbles.'

And Cassandra replied on her Tumblr, 'Yes, Grandma, yes.'

A Masculine Trilemma

Later, after I moved to this rusted city, I sent Cassandra my novel about online dating. I thought then, she must have forgotten about not having the bubbles, because she posted the cover of my novel, along with a picture of her coffee on her curated social media. Cassandra must have then remembered the paucity of bubbles because she never responded to comments from curious others.

Now from before a long wooden table I see the photo of Helena on a tropical beach. Still there, years later, her tan legs and a page of my novel about online dating. In her post, Helena wrote my name and #getit, before she found the part with a composite of an MFA friend in her cohort, Adriana. Helena messaged me, asking about 'how much' of the novel about online dating was 'true.' I emailed back an evasive answer, knowing Helena to be a poet, thinking we understood art.

She never replied.

Maybe if I thought about flamingos now, how they only go on our clothes now. Our appetites are too much, I mean, all these liquids and meats and creams cram down our inexhaustible mouths. Our holes and members, those too can never have enough rubbing, jamming, sucking. The standard Christ imbued in us is an internal temperature of an upright bipedal form. Not too hairy. Not too manicured either, not too bereft of primordial foliage sprouting from oozing genitals.

These ideas, my wife gets bored when I tell her on the green couch during our weekends together. She finishes my sentences like a schoolteacher helping a child.

Christ, I know I should be brasher, like a man at Lion's Head in the 1970s. But how, when I do not even hold court at staid small plates restaurants with my wife's doctor friends? Their work terminology passes by me harmlessly.

Gardner said you are supposed to be the expert in every discipline, and I am not a master of my own past. What I ate for breakfast is a mystery, and here I am before a long wooden table thinking of a conversation from the other night, when I talked with another former friend, in the South. An awkward pause came after talking about old flings. He was nostalgic, I think, so I jumped in and offered the only reason he loved Chicago, as it reminded him of being, 'So deep in so many hipsters' mouths.'

'Yeah,' he said, giggling. 'That's true.'

Quips leave me regretful, so all I can do now is recite my dream from last night. The man who sang about rented rooms pointed to Audrina, on a hillside working on her bicycle. Falling into my arms, Audrina recalled our month together in Minneapolis. In the dream we lived near a gated field by an encampment of trailers. Mountains, a barrage of missiles blacking the sky, and Audrina said, 'Should we get back together?'

Now before going to the cubicle I looked up Audrina's latest tweets. Before I met her Audrina attended private schools her whole life, yet her feed is about the privilege *of others*. Before we met, she bragged to me about her 'great big ass.' After our night of karaoke in Nordeast, she showed me. More impressive was her body odor on my mattress on the floor.

The next morning, the last time I saw her, leaving my Malibu. I dropped Audrina off that winter morning at her brother's place. She lived in his basement. That cold Minneapolis morning she wore flip top mittens, the sun was blinding, and she gave me a kiss on the cheek. I was full of love. What a fool.

BEFORE A LONG WOODEN TABLE XI

For deep down beneath it all is the gloomy feeling, not to be repressed, that all this hectic zeal is the despairing self-deception of a soul that may not and cannot rest
-Spengler

On Albert, not Mango, we had no tubs of lard. Papa did not go to the neighbors for buckets of water. I did not receive leering looks from the cholos. Now, I think, before this long wooden table, if only I had felt the heavy thumb of the whites, my books of vanity could be saved from anonymity, given covers with titles written in cursive above a geometric shape made from a Spirograph. Roulette curves, I know as someone who wants his books to be plain but beautiful, so the words inside seem important. And again I am hungry.

Nearby me now are grunting others who do not worry about anything other than how to stream their digital content. I type in a minimized window, after listening to a manager wail to me about needing to divorce. On her trip to the copier, she stopped and leaned over my cubicle, told me how *her husband* is the one with the substance abuse problem. Arms resting over my wall, she admitted she blew positive for alcohol on the morning her husband swatted a phone out of her hands.

'You can bet your ass I called the cops,' the manager told me. I said something like 'man,' and she left me to this.

My coworkers now discuss dog grooming, as I ruminate on destruction. On my long walk to work today a pickup barreled down an exit and rammed into the back of a small car. For the rest of the walk past the fairgrounds I chided myself for not preventing the accident.

Before leaving the scene, I walked by the tall man who drove the pickup. He went over and stood by the small car, peered in, asked if everyone

87

was okay. A large woman in the passenger seat jumped in her seat, making the small car rock, and yelled, 'Why the fuck you hit us from the back, motherfucker!' While a phlegmatic man in the driver's seat told his woman, 'Calm down, bitch.'

Now in the cubicle I reach back on my head and feel my rubbery scalp, like an ugly dying, and I know Christ smites me.

Throw the spear, Christ, down toward a cubicle on a former factory floor where it smells of sour eggs from the fast food my greasy-haired coworker inhales. He stays thin, no matter what, and I too want to be sleek. More so I would like to not be waylaid each morning scrolling through photos of fitness influencers who advertise content I never buy but consider buying.

Christ, what I mean is You made me not the one I saw slide in and out of a Latina this morning, so oiled and immense. Desiccated and decreasing, I did not move a bumper to the side of the road, and today is only Wednesday.

BEFORE A LONG WOODEN TABLE XII

And if we work out all this well and carefully,
And the husband lives with us and lightly bears his yoke,
This life is enviable. If not, I'd rather die
- Euripides

A text last night, telling me to download a new app.

Hiding my phone's screen away from my sleeping wife in bed, I fiddled with the inscrutable features, thinking of Kaliyah sending me messages of her Amazonian form. Built like she could play in a woman's lingerie football league, Kaliyah met with me at the dive bar, where I gave her my books. Nothing ever happened.

We met because we did not want to be forgotten. She wanted to know she was still viable, and I wanted someone to tell me I was right to spend all this time remembering. I continue before a long wooden table.

Once, I kissed hefty teardrops. The next morning in the rented attic an online dater left her bra beside the mattress on the floor. Enamored with her auburn hair and hairy mons, I bought her a stuffed owl at my job at a corporate bookstore, but she never came back for her expensive underwear. That private college graduate lived as a hippie in Seward, drank PBRs, took a bath once a week, and never came back.

Or the collage artist, Adelina. She wore gray sweatpants and a Carleton sweatshirt for our afternoon of watching reality TV. On my mattress on the floor Adelina asked me, 'Do you wanna sideways 69?' in a way, I thought at the time, that signaled she had learned the position in Northfield and was sure it was best. Two weeks later, Adelina's texted: 'Things are just getting too relationshipy.'

Then the high school basketball star. By the time we met she had become a staff member for *Quadrangle*, the status creative writing blog in Minneapolis. She found my dating profile and messaged to go out for 'beers over what we're writing.' I said yes, 'of course, yes.'

In Uptown we went from Mexican food and margaritas to walking while smoking cigarettes (I did not smoke) to watching a band of flannel guys playing outside a bar I would have never stopped at normally but with the high school basketball star it seemed natural. We held hands to her place by the interstate and ate pizza, watched a movie with her gay roommate. In the morning she whispered in my ear, 'See you soon,' and closed her apartment door with its stickers for leftist causes. I never saw her again.

Now before this long wooden table I remember I thought *I am going bald* at 20, when I had a full head of hair. At 30 I was sure I was fat, when I was thirty pounds lighter than I am now. Our self-image is distorted, I say before a long wooden table for no one, until we reach an age when we stop trying to discern its shape. A quick swipe of the steam, to see if we bleed; that's enough.

And still I want the private college graduates I once knew to emerge from the closets and appliances in this crumbling duplex, as Todd's women did in the music video for "48 Roses."

Last night, I could add, I drank vodka on the green couch. When my wife went to bed I watched a video of a Middle Eastern woman in a hijab, experimenting with the Western world. This morning I cleared my history, poured out the alcohol, shaved my head and thought to pray but did not. Now, I think before this long wooden table, if I sent my thoughts to Allah, could I be known? So well the baristas from the coffee shop over the weekend would have recognized me?

They made coffee in a gleaming boutique roaster in these cheesy suburbs. On the walk back to the crumbling duplex I tamped the urge to comment on them, knowing, even if we laughed, a residual knowledge would hang: I had brought up the baristas, who to my wife were likely forgettable but to me the busty pale one pushed out of her white tank top as if trying to ascend to heaven, while the plain Asian looked as if she could devour a man.

My whole morning is wasted, trying to recover from this foggy haze. Blood breaks down the poisons. In my youth I could wake and be groggy until I took a shower and ate greasy food, but I did nothing with those Saturdays other than pine over Greer. In those ineffectual times I could at least get on my feet and not spend the day convalescing, like today before going to the cubicle, spent skimming through a hot new novel by another hot new writer.

A hollow thing, something the short-banged author wrote from an enclave. A corporation paid her an advance for words that will make nothing happen. It will give a vacationer on an expensive beach something to use as a status symbol, and that nothing is something I want badly. My epistles of wanting are never going to be published.

I should forget my dreams and subscribe to *The Important Review of Books*, have people over for a living, and when confronted with the problem of citizens living as political prisoners in America, I will say: '*Those people* shouldn't have voted for *that guy.*'

The elite sons and daughters never sent my stories to the next rung, I repeat, but those privileged neonates rightfully blocked my path, as all I can think about before this long wooden table is the big box store employee from the other morning.

I imagine us now on a farm, where I work as a poet, the big box store employee does online influencing, and my wife gardens.

Our third wore brown pants, a red shirt, and unpacked boxed noodles wearing glasses and a Wisconsin t-shirt with the state symbol. Hair in two tight braids, she was too much for my heart, so I left for the cooler. She had small breasts I missed dearly, so I wandered back to her aisle. When I returned, the way her pants hugged her thighs, Christ, I thought of the big box store employee religiously, and needed to escape to the next aisle again. By the time I got back I saw her leaving in khaki pants like tights, and her shirt rode up barely. I needed to sit down. I found a barren aisle and rested, sick with jealousy. The holy one drifted out of my life and back for her senior year of college, then to Asheville, I imagined as I finished my shopping.

By how she stocked the boxed noodles, I wanted her more than food. I should be trying to write a novel about her, yet I keep thinking about how my kind must jump into a volcano and now again the one who shelved boxed noodles with a subtle midriff, glasses, a welcoming face, and put away boxed noodles better than I have ever seen anyone put away boxed noodles.

I could add, last night alone on the green couch, I watched a man pump hard, causing a normal-looking woman to wobble erratically. This morning I wanted to look her up. Instead I purged myself in the shower and the desire dissipated, I went to the long wooden table and turned on my computer. I began to wonder about the big box employee.

Please, Christ, have a technology company wipe my words.

My AI work is saving the world, the tech executive says to himself, hopping off his private jet on the cliffs of Big Sur before going inside his mansion to be fed confit by a nude Swedish masseuse in a Finnish sauna. I know those luxuries are a simulacrum of what our modern lords do with their billions. Me, I would buy the wool Mackinaw Cruiser to stay warm in Bellingham, so I could find Greer, yet I would never find her. She moved back home to Minnesota. I think she got married.

BEFORE A LONG WOODEN TABLE XIII

> Come on, Catullus!
> Be obstinately obdurate!
> - *Catullus*

'*...there will always be strength and freedom in knowing what you want,'* wrote Yates, or Mates, as I called him in a story I will publish myself, I worry.

My only original thought this morning comes in knowing why I wanted in the rented attic. My job at the generic pharmaceutical factory made me dirty. That filth forced the one opposite me in the pho booth to extricate herself through texts like: 'I am soooo sorry. Just not looking for a *whole thing* right now.'

Was wrong to blame steelyards, factories, now a cubicle near the fairgrounds, where I will be next to resentful cases working for the social good, as they tell us, when really we work to benefit our bald CEO with chicken legs. Orange tan, he walks around like, 'He knows he's good-looking,' I was told by a coworker.

Shocking, to hear that. Later, in the awful stillness of my cubicle, not as much. Power, the black SUV he drives, that must have wetted her in her cube. Soon in mine, I will be regretting the day I came out of the womb. I do not preach eugenics, other than the neutering of my sensitive kind. Nurture those who jump high, are good at math, and never worry of what they will be when they grow up, as that is 'for *homos.*'

This is as fey as a feather, the opposite weight of my body, yet I keep eating in this crumbling duplex, so I will never work as a thin professor at a private college, and in my office spank fresh undergraduates with sporty thighs. I keep writing for those imaginary ones, why, when no one cares about this kind of thing anymore except for a fraction of educated white women, and only so they can tear the author of a made-up story down. I never used the phrase 'toxic masculinity' correctly, so I never found a foothold in their Important Creative world. Instead I tweeted: 'All male feminists are misogynists,' and ended up in these cheesy suburbs, yearning for assignations with waitresses from the other weekend in Madison, at the restaurant with windows for walls. Hearty fairies worked there, each one under the effects of the same tranquil drug, it seemed, as they looked like they were floating around with their trays, ample asses and easy smiles. They appeared ready to join a harem for a vested man with an excellent job and a deep grasp of the scriptures.

Here, without, each night in the crumbling duplex my wife will sense I am dreaming of the hearty fairies whose job was to smile and walk in high-waisted jeans and have hypnotizing faces and big asses.

After we left the restaurant with the peaceful waitresses, I spotted a toned Asian, walking into a yoga studio. I stared at her, I thought inconspicuously, though I am sure my wife saw me looking. I could not help it. The toned Asian wore short spandex shorts that could not contain her. As we drove home, I imagined that toned Asian going to herbal stretching class, never worrying of anything but her farmer's market on Saturday where she buys her stinky cheese and fresh thongs. Now, before this long wooden table, I want to say, that the muscled nymph's religion is hedonism. I want to submit to the coming power and have five wives with untroubled minds and sporty asses that thud each night creating beautiful vibrations.

Christ, help me forget my dreams and concentrate on how to condition myself to run through these cheesy suburbs until exhaustion. If lithe, I could become an Important Creative in charge of literature contests, thumping hopefuls in the face with my power.

A Masculine Trilemma

This is all distraction before going to the cubicle. I should be transforming three days of a family vacation in the Dells, the stop in Madison was on the way home. After we returned to the crumbling duplex my wife and I argued so much we both cried. She left in her Subaru and did not return for hours. If someone paid me to record everything, I would tell them of my failures. Instead, before this long wooden table, I just saw an artful Spanish woman, breasts like torpedoes. We will never cross paths, that tanlined Spanish woman, not unless she moves here and becomes a client at my social work job. Our dalliance would get me fired, then I would be hopeless, in Hartland. I want to write for a living, I say before this long wooden table. I may as well want to hula-hoop.

My genes should be phased out, these genes which inspire me to lust over a Spanish woman, and now one in California eating a big carrot who looks up and down after a bite and captions the post, 'Now that's a carrot.' In another clip she spanks the unblemished ass of a friend on a Malibu beach, squeezes until eliciting a giggle. The clip abruptly ends.

My wife has no time for carrot-eaters and their friends who have sand in their fit creases.

To forget the pain, I watched a French woman reading the part in *The Loser* where Glenn wants to be the Steinway. And I am good at that, at watching a French woman read Bernhard and reach apotheosis.

After, in the cold hush, looking in the bathroom mirror, I wondered, are men not supposed to become more successful with age? If that is not true for me, on what can I rely? Vanity presses publishing me, balding, and dying?

Back at the long wooden table now, birds sing near the rickety windows. Out in the Dells, dark waters rush through flat layers of rock. As someone who, when he lived in Cascadia, called himself a Gnostic hedonist, I paste drafts, hoping something will come of this trying, something other than dust.

Black Elk and how his story mirrors Plato's Cave. Those 70s swim shorts with the line down the thigh. Gallimard wanting my work. A woman masturbating after reading ethics by Baruch. To be as immortal of a lover poet as D'Annuzino. A modern version of Peter Paul's Three Graces modeled by three models with thighs as juicy as drumsticks and rumps as delectable as hams.

BEFORE A LONG WOODEN TABLE XIV

Is there any peace
In ever climbing up the climbing wave?
-Tennyson

When I lived in a rented attic I started a literature and culture website and called it Good Clean Blog. I had people I knew write essays and reviews. I even made a social media profile and a logo. In that same time I housed my short stories at what I called 30 Sad Stories. Nothing happened, so I started another blog complaining about my life, and called that Dumb Sad Blog. Later, on another blog called Every Word I Have Written, I wrote critiques of my own writing. Before that I made what I called The Story Project, typing commissioned stories on a typewriter in my rented attic. Frustrated by its failure I wrote a post on my personal website where I derided Alt Lit authors. One found my obscure post and commented, 'Hmm, I see,' as if saying: *All the ripe asses you were supposed to kiss are not going to bend over for you.* For years I put my work up at *Feeling Magazine*, thinking something good would happen by uploading to their 'all thinking matters' servers. Over and over I put my name in the ignoble places that are meant to get you noticed by the average places that are supposed to lead you to real publications.

I did so many things, I say before a long wooden table, though none would have been as effective as simply being born as someone who is noticed. I strove to be as well-known as an adjunct creative writing professor at a public university.

To be even a bearded piss boy I would need to get divorced then remarried, have my new marriage announcement published in *the New York Times*, and that same year release a novel about leaving my husband and later hitchhiking to meet up with someone in New Zealand and in interviews with literature publications talk about how I went to New Zealand in real life and hitchhiked in real life and now I am living with my new husband in Chicago who writes postmodern novels and teaches at the art school and have the temerity to say my work is not autobiographical. I need to have the audaciousness to lie.

An example of modern ethics would be to say, 'Please, algorithm, send more me stories about racism.'

At least now I am distracted by a Belgian with long curly hair. Thinking of a Wisconsinite who once won Miss Teen will not help the pain, even if I just saw that the Wisconsinite is full and healthy, with a tomboy who has grown into a woman look. Thinking of the aloof Californian who eats carrots will not help. Nor will thinking of one on a fashion blog with a gap tooth. Thinking of her, that sturdy model doing a handstand in a black bodysuit next to a houseplant, will not take me further. I could keep going with those I have found online and would become polygamous with, if my wife allowed it, creatures who contain a primal nature that could inspire me to fight, if there were ever a just war.

Good thick women started me this Monday morning when I should be on my knees, praying to not yearn for their roundness. I should be fasting, hoping the fanaticism makes me into a zealot who cares only about supplicating to Important Creatives. Never again want pointed breasts, wild bushes, fat backsides.

Every night in the crumbling duplex I talk with my wife about her work. Never do I talk to her about those I find in my scrolling, Rose or Eugenie, Aurora or Peach or Emily or Tessa or Carianne, or Elena, who entered my dreams before light broke this morning.

Birds chirping, I dreamed I peed myself. Opening my eyes, I felt come sliding down my hip, and with the dripping I knew I had the same outlook and was alone.

98

A Masculine Trilemma

Now I write about that which I want to slap and suck, to spite the celebrators of death, the Important Creatives who tweet like slaveowners from their lofts in Brooklyn.

One group I will never find pity for are the meth addicts in Portland waving flags of *resistance*, so they can get into the pants of high school girls with patchouli-soaked dreads. We should castrate those men. Libidos rule them, as mine did when I believed every word of *Loose Change*. Back in middle aughts I thought everyone should give their wealth away, as Christ instructed us to. If only I had been a eunuch.

A decade after apostatizing, I remember when I first published myself, a novel about online dating. I told everyone, even old Christian friends in Cascadia. Elena was one. For her I recently sent a link to my secret blog where I post videos of expressive women reading in artistic undress. She never responded. I too should have been castrated. I would not now be wanting Christian women I once knew to send new pictures of their impressive curves. All this explains the domestic tension.

I wonder now from before a long wooden table, what would the fights be about if I worked at a job where I controlled hundreds? All my woman would ever get mad about is when she would say, 'How come you didn't take my ass for an hour like you did with Rebecca the other night?'

Our spats forgotten with an unzipping and a lifting. Brutish, yes, yet I know as that man I would never be told I am not 'defending' my wife. No one cuts the well-earning hog that sates. Sensitivities would be kept inside.

As a way of staying servile, all this morning I have contemplated buying a game with a Greek god protagonist. I bought nothing and went outside, took a big dead limb on our street and threw it in the hinterland between our garage and neighbor's garage, filled with clumps of grass from when the teen boy mowed. The single mother downstairs also has a busty teen who goes out in the yard with cut-off shirts.

Instead of wallowing like Humbert I should go over my story about rejected stories, but whenever I get the slightest notion to try, I am punished with cannonballs of doubt, and that metaphor is another reason why I will never be known, except to my wife, who is sad her husband wanders, and my parents, who worry I am going to hell, and old Christian friends, who do not want to read my vain attempts.

Worse, I have grown callous, like this morning on the way inside the crumbling duplex I came upon a drying worm on the sidewalk. Once, I know, I would have reached down and picked up the grasping thing. That tender spirit was gone. I smashed down until the worm became like the shredded mash left on a cutting board, and now a big truck pulls up to our street. Our psychotic landlord may have put that limb there to be carried away. How was I to know? How was I to know anything?

And still there is Leila, and the pasty yoga instructor with red hair in love with crystals, and a blonde journalist with a mouth that could eat a man. From before this long wooden table I declare I want them to sit their big asses on my face. Christ does not make His children equal, I say before a long wooden table. Some are to desire while others are to be desiring.

Soon, my wife will return to this upper level for lunch, and I will need to be as palpitated to have her as I would be if I were about to lick Leila. The conundrum of monogamy is just this: to feel a longtime partner as you would feel someone new.

And now I am resisting the urge to search for Greer, and to revisit where I lived in Sioux Falls, down the street from the post-religious Christians. Before I moved west, I smoked ditch weed in their basement, of a shared house off Phillips Ave. In that dank basement girls wearing skirts over tights sat Indian style on the floor next to guys with beards before guys with beards. They had tattoos and wanted more tattoos. We listened to Jenny Lewis and talked about how bad George Bush was.

A Masculine Trilemma

Now the desire returns, for a Belgian with long curly hair, but writing about that desire is not a job. I hear men across the street cut down branches for a living. Christ does not allocate evenly, I say again, as there is a movie star in a green dress on the beach, and underneath her colorful sari she is jasmine and lavender, with a warmth that would open a man's third eye.

Or again, I give in, is Leila, who in a clip belts a phallus around her head and playfully slaps her German friend in the face. Then comes a challenge. Leila does more, downing a whole banana, while her German friend can barely get halfway. Leila glides the white fruit in and out of her mouth, giggling, like she could never be unhappy.

BEFORE A LONG WOODEN TABLE XV

And vile and unclean as I was, so great was my vanity that I was bent upon passing for clean and courtly.

-Augustine

Now in the disturbing quiet before leaving for the cubicle I know my books will never be read by anyone outside those I force my writings upon, so I will never luck into a job that would encourage a creative writing minor on a sports scholarship to be with me and one of her friends, and I am bad at math and will never work my way into one of those positions, and I am balding and think of what Pavese said in his journal:

'No words. An act. I won't write anymore.'

I did not want to die in adolescence when Joy gave me the note, written by Stacy, about why we had to break up. No details remain other than Stacy saying she *cried* as she wrote. Not until much later, after online dating in Minneapolis, did I understand the only way to end things was by lying. As a boy on the plains, I wanted to live.

My senior year of high school, braces taken off, I was friends with arty kids from the private school and I played football. I had gone through my growth spurt, at last becoming as tall as the other boys in my class who started to grow in the 7th grade when they put creatine in their water and lifted so much that by senior year they had pecs bigger than the breasts of the girls in our class. I attended a brick church in the country and did not believe guilt should be associated with God. A Jewish man from the Iron Age did not make me go bald each time I yearned to see a naked woman. I did not want death, but my lack of direction, I see now, lead me to searching for love. By not ever finding it, a dissonance arose, thoughts of death encroached.

At my land grant university that first year I pounded my fists on a lofted bed, as if a Swedish man directed me for a scene exemplifying the pain of someone who suffered a great loss. I had lost no one. At the end of my first year, I had not found The One. Her absence was my lamentation. I pounded my mattress in anguish, how I would have desire but be without. I called out to God and heard silence.

The next year I called out to Him after my limp prick brushed against a nude thigh. My almost-first swore like a sailor and boasted the kind of domineering body I did not want then but would grow to. We had climbed up to her lofted bed after a keg party in another dorm. A poster of Leo above us as she worked. Before she set herself down, I thought of an excuse.

'I need to get up early,' I said, squirming out from under her significance.

A flowery, rank scent following me, I hustled out to her mumbling expletives, worrying as I went up the concrete stairs that she would become pregnant by my limp prick grazing against her.

Back in my dorm room, I prayed. I prayed and began to feel that Christ came up with the get-up-early excuse. He gave me the bravery. Certain I was heard, up in my own lofted bed I asked Christ into my heart, and I remember the rush, like a ghost entering me.

BEFORE A LONG WOODEN TABLE XVI

God's mercy is strange,
its mystery crushing
-Prado

Real thoughts of death began when I started to believe. I lived alone in an all-guys dorm my third year, I lacquered my walls with posters of bands like Owls, made mixtapes for girls in my religious group, dyed my hair blonde, wore black, went to classes to complete a journalism minor. Never did I invest in my major of psychology and teaching. I pursued the hereafter, spending the summer evangelizing in Colorado.

And desire built up like calcium deposits. It was sin, I knew, to want a girlfriend before marriage. I had read the abstinence books. If a man looked at a woman with lust, he was worthy of hell.

My last year at the land grant university, with a position as the music director of the radio station, I had access to a computer with internet, so, every Saturday morning I strolled the quiet campus to the student union. Descending into the bowels, past the spacious newspaper office to our tiny office with the pink Mac, I would key in the password and pour over women in *Playboy* galleries. Spill onto the carpeted floor, clean up with a brown paper towel, and trudge back to the showers in the men-only dorm. While other guys slept, water fell on my back, and I knew my hair fell out: Christ sought retribution.

After student teaching in a small town my final semester, I left for Texas, for a summer internship at a Christian music magazine called *God Metal*. That summer I housesat for a Mennonite couple who left behind a boxy desktop computer. No longer did I need to walk to another building. I could shuffle carpeted steps in an air-conditioned home and admire a woman (most of her work locked behind a paywall) who looked like someone I knew back home, Sheena, with dark straight hair.

After indulging, I would go to the shower, where I would pray for the wanting to be taken away. Christ did not hear me, I thought, in anguish, and often could not sleep.

My eyes must have looked dead. That summer, one of the other interns at the Christian music magazine asked me if I was dealing with, as he called it, 'a secret sin.'

The summer before, in Colorado, I devoted all my free time to the scriptures. On walks I listened to Stavesacre on my Discman. I read and I prayed to Christ to take away the wanting, while around me my peers fondled each other in the dark. Every Saturday, before we went out proselytizing downtown, I would shave my head. Blood flowing down my neck in the cramped shower, I would be glad: I needed a physical sign to show Him my abnegation of nudity. No matter how much skin I scrapped off, I was sure Christ chose me to hang from a tree like Judas.

I must have looked like I wanted to drown when my father visited the basement apartment in Vermilion. I lived there after college with my brother-in-law's brother, David, who had majored in art and grew up in a family where everyone else had figured out their lives. As the youngest, like me, David wanted to be a creative. That year I watched David pine for a sprinter who attended the same religious meetings on campus. One night, I remember, she came over to our basement apartment and David and I laughed about it later, how David warmed pizza bites in the oven as a romantic gesture. David was sensitive and prone to fall for fit Christian girls with muscular legs who went for older guys who left fit Christian girls perplexed as to why they were always getting their hearts broken.

I did not tell my dad any of that. After earning a degree in psychology at the land grant university, I worked as an in-school suspension supervisor in Sioux Falls. I must have looked aimless. The sun set as my dad looked at me square in the eye.

'It doesn't seem like you have any direction,' he said.

The smell of fecund dirt through the basement windowsill, and I thought, *I can't tell you, Dad, that I have ending thoughts.* I could not tell my dad the creator of the universe orchestrated my balding.

'I'm trying,' I said, and my father left that garden level apartment as disappointed as he came.

A reason for living came soon after, in Nebraska. I found a job as a houseparent, leading delinquent teenagers to Christ. The plan was to use the setting in the isolated town as a solitary temple only devoted searchers could find. *I will achieve purification here*, I thought then, and resolved to not look at naked women in Playboy photo galleries. To help, I put my CRT monitor in the carpeted kitchen of the house I shared with the other two male houseparents.

That focus lasted a week. Elna arrived. Elna played volleyball at a private college in Iowa and she laughed at my jokes. One of the teen boys at the group home said she looked like 'the *Tomb Raider* girl.'

Elna kept me devout. For hours every day of that year I called upon Christ's will. I was sure I heard His voice when, at the end of that year, Elna agreed to a date in Grand Island.

In Grand Island we ate Mexican food, we watched a new movie called *Ron Burgundy*, where I saw her eyes lit up in the dark theater. After the movie I drove us back on the interstate to the group home. A Death Cab for Cutie song played as Elna fell into sleep, or pretended to.

A month later she left three days earlier than she said she would be leaving and the only time I heard from Elna again is when she replied to my email. I had sent her a message, asking if she received the care package I sent to her new place of work, at a library in Iowa. She wrote at the end: '…focus on Christ, Henry, not on me.'

A Masculine Trilemma

I had to move away from the group home, from the clean roads, the blades of grass, all of that which reminded me of my spiritual weakness, so I went home. After a month with my parents, mostly playing a fantasy game called *Sorrowgale* and eating free food, I found a group home job in Sioux Falls, and a studio apartment behind Sunshine Foods.

Often I went on walks to the public library and read alongside homeless Natives. That's when I found the graphic novel, *Sweaters*, about growing up religious and finding and losing The One. *Sweaters* mirrored my life, I thought, and wondered if I might be an artist too, so I wrote a story about a guy reflecting on losing the love of his life because of his lack of faith while walking to the library in a blizzard. Days later, my bulky desktop computer died. I did not try again for some time.

A year later, I lived in the upper level of a house in McKennan Park. A year since Elna, and I was beginning to see the only reason I believed was to have a powerful matchmaker. Then, like a miracle, faith restored. Christ found her on Myspace, a thrower named Susannah in Mississippi. We talked every day. Within a month I was in bliss in the South, in her one-room apartment inside of a mansion. Below floorboards, in a coffin for a bedroom, Susannah showed me the best way, by rubbing my prick's head on her sensitivity while she put her finger inside herself. In her shower I watched in awe as she used the attachment nozzle on herself like a magic wand. Christ singled Susannah out as a consolation prize, is what I thought. Three days passed like three seconds. The morning I returned to Sioux Falls, a text.

'You are just not a good spiritual leader, Henny. We can't see each other again.'

So I quit my jobs and drove west to Cascadia, where I did not know sin when those recently graduated from private colleges gave me massages in my rented room inside a commune house called Praxis. Life's goal was to feel good in that bedroom twinkling with Christmas lights, inside of a house I

107

found through Christian friends from Sioux Falls. Not long into that time I backed my white Taurus into a truck on a crowded street, gouging its door, and for the remaining years in Cascadia I had thoughts of death, jolted back to how I left a note but never resolved the issue with the owner.

Instead of Christ, I was sure Fate punished me, never allowing me to move up at my job in package distribution, making me dumb enough to watch Greer go to Bellingham without telling her my truest feelings. I moved back to the Middle West, to the frozen suburbs of Minneapolis, where I online date, started a personal website, and worked at factories. Later, I moved to the neighboring state, got married, and published a novel about online dating. Now smoky neighbors live downstairs, making grunts in the night, and I work in a cubicle and publish books about my life for no one. Later, after I move again, from these cheesy suburbs to racist suburbs outside a cold black city of death, I will finish my last book.

PART III

THE HOUSEHUSBAND

I cannot afford to believe that freedom from intolerance is the right of only one particular group
-Lorde

THE HOUSEHUSBAND I

Discretion, ever more discretion, learn to be wrong. The world is full of people who are right.
That's why it is so revolting

- Céline

Now outside a cold black city of death in the racist suburbs (I have finished graduate school in the arts and am a househusband before a cheap Target desk in a square, unfurnished room, as the long wooden table is in a living room, used more by my wife and baby) I know three truths:

1. One must treat each person as one would want to be treated.

2. No one can see into another heart.

3. Bullying someone for how they were born is bullying.

Economics, and the vicissitudes which create those economic conditions, play a role in man's goodness, yet one must deny anyone who frames violent rhetoric as *progress*. Reject those Satanists, I say before a cheap Target desk. Cleave anyone who mandates one must adopt fundamentalism, not in the religion of youth (which I can now say, years apart from its intense zenith, at least had value, giving art, laws, civilization) but in the religion of progress, which is a hollow one, full of apparatchiks.

Never have I been appointed for anything, so I do not fear the mobs. I welcome them. As was said: 'For the worst thing you can do to an author is to be silent as to his works.' So I welcome the paid terrorists, in the streets this summer shouting the gospel of original sin. They may cozy next to me as I declare from before a cheap Target desk that anyone who says one's color and gonads need purification are weaklings inured with soft brains used for creating more power for the already powerful.

111

Spot them, those youthful demons indoctrinated by wealthy parents who inoculated their child from incrimination of thought impurity, or the demon was born poor and found that unfair, so they reached out to a State which promised safety and bounties for their guerrilla service, or the demon in part of the gilded class whose job it is now to appear guilty, feign empathy, and go about receiving money for creating division.

Brands participate in the pantomime too. I say from before this cheap Target desk, one must not care about brands or others, only about making, even if there is no real community.

As long ago, a man said, 'the literary scene is a Medusa's raft, small and sinking.' Now the raft is an inflatable on fire and to get on the plastic dinghy, one must dive to the bottom of the ocean, swimming past other yearning sharks, and there apologize for his inherent badness, only to resurface to the melting lifeboat, to tell the people on board, 'I have dived down and apologized for my badness,' and while treading water pray the three bobbing on the makeshift boat believe.

They will not, I know as a househusband in the racist suburbs, or they may, but they will say they do not, so one must dive down again to the bottom and apostatize.

Do this again and again, until drowning.

THE HOUSEHUSBAND II

Who does not obey shall not eat
- *Trotsky*

This morning, before continuing from before a cheap Target desk, a bug man came to our house in these racist suburbs. After I answered the door, a masked Mormon stood before me and preached: 'You need to buy our magic dust...'

I heard, did not listen, thinking of a way to get the Mormon off our porch. After minutes of haranguing, the Mormon got his opportunity. My wife came to the front door with our baby, and the masked Mormon said, 'So *she* must be the decision maker.'

Now, as I sit before a cheap Target desk, a masked Mormon sprays magic dust around our house in these racist suburbs.

Only living far away from everyone is good, I know before this cheap Target desk, unable to tell my wife I want to disappear. I go on, hoping *something nice* will happen, when all will happen is the child terrorists dressed in black, this summer burning those who oppose them, will one day deride the new, younger group of terrorists 'who aren't even as violent as we were, when we were changing things in this country *for good.*'

Watching hypocrisy blossom is the only good thing now.

But the process is so slow. One must wait and watch through socialist teens and twenties, democratic socialist thirties, moves to racist suburbs, promotions at hateful jobs, all so the aging hypocrites can support children they love, as those children will be born a way the aging hypocrites will no longer be able to say is wrong.

Waiting for bad ideology to erode takes time.

Nothing is good in the immediate. I am not successful enough to have affairs, so I cannot be what a man is supposed to be, as the German philosopher said, 'a bigamist.' Or, as was said by another man, 'A lasting relationship with a woman is only possible if you are a business failure.'

As a chaste failure in the racist suburbs, I am dumbfounded by the easy callousness with which self-named 'empaths' employ name-calling online.

All this after returning from the Clearing without Pirandello. Arriving at noon, I went up to the library entrance, only to see a man in the window lifting a sign that said, 'Open at 2:00.' My wife and baby waited in the car, so I turned back to my wife's car and drove us to these racist suburbs without Pirandello. Now before a cheap Target desk I want to *feel heat from all the bodies,* the warmth of a fitness influencer, but that cannot be in these racist suburbs where the households of rectitude place platitudes in their yards. Passing by on walks with my little one, I always think: *Amazing, these winds, these grasses and trees, they are real.*

And still I want to be a man in one of those houses of morals. As a champion of business, at night in my office with ruddy interns, they will think it fun to watch a married man crawl on the floor. Giggling, the young curly-haired intern will look back to see an old man eating from their fresh backside that is trembling and wobbling with hope, for *a fun summer.*

A Masculine Trilemma

THE HOUSEHUSBAND III

Marriage is a form of servitude for man also
- de Beauvoir

Throughout history, I know before a cheap Target desk, men have been the greatest writers. As men, throughout history, have been driven to know rounder asses, more pert titties. Those men would not have known those parts any other way, so they stayed in a quiet room and conjured ideas, to impress a form of *20 or so years*.

In the racist suburbs I can also say this computer program, whenever I write 'nymphet,' tells me to consider omitting. I change nothing, not because I am obstinate, but because I have no readers who would get offended. Make no mistake; I am a coward. I would change every single word if an Important Creative editor in Brooklyn told me to.

Also, I can say before this cheap Target desk, I hate when I give perfect quotes and the one I am talking with over the phone, instead of complimenting my knowledge, talks over me to disagree, like last night.

'Valery said a poem is never finished, only abandoned,' I said to a guy named Jay over the phone. He replied, 'Well, Valery was a fascist.'

Jay, white and straight, is too hurt to agree with anyone, so he left the cold black city of death after our two years of graduate school in the arts and went back in Texas to be a pretend communist. Jay always told me he was sober, after bragging in the graduate lounge about how much weed he smoked, because, as Jay said, 'only alcohol can ruin your life.'

All of us will die with falseness in our hearts, some more than others. The bad ones can be spotted in these ways: if a man is unable to imagine himself in the ostracized position as the person he is accusing of heretical behavior, a

115

man is dissonant. If a man is convinced some are born morally capable and that judgement is made along someone's immutable characteristics, a man is dissonant. If a man thinks gathering in large groups is justified, if the cause for the gathering aligns with their causes, a man is dissonant. If a man equivocates violence to allay the responsibility of his political affiliation, a man is dissonant. If a man is unable to agree with anyone he views as aesthetically lower, a man is dissonant.

Foxworthy I am not, only a househusband in racist suburbs, but I am sure that the strength of a man's spirit is measured by how many of those axioms he can tolerate, to what extent he needs to have them 'diluted, disguised, sweetened, muted, falsified.'

My truth is I just purged all my likes and follows, after suddenly realizing I hated not only our virus lords who preach violence for progress but also the pragmatists who want *classic liberalism* to return. Those Important Creatives, neck-bearded chubby ones with book deals and blue checkmarks, say they want to hear 'all viewpoints.' I hate those Important Creatives, as they do not allow me onto their Important and Creative raft.

Not friends with privately educated progressives or the paid terrorists in the streets burning elk for progress, I know the burning is insane, but everything is, including graduate schools with creative writing programs. The professors there take students' money and in return give promises. Worse, the aging students are so wanting they drink those promises as if they drink nutritive milk.

One of my professors, Jim, who I gave my books to (and he later gave them away, as I found through backchannel sources) chokes on his artifice. Not because he gave away my books, but because everything he says is a lie, to save himself. Jim has avoided the mobs so far, as Jim was ushered into his position. In the Before Time, Jim wrote novels about the different ways he *fingered punk girls* in the back of his 'old man's car...and she smelled of cigarettes and her patchouli shampoo,' and it was fine, even beloved. Now Jim writes apologia, as Jim wants to keep his job where he preys on halfsies who were 'so honored' to have received an email in their second week at graduate school, asking if they were 'doing okay' after one day of looking mopey in our seminar on the history of the novel.

Jim would deny he wanted that halfsie, or that he gave away my books, but Jim is a liar, no better or worse than the rest of us. For our sin of being born this way, we will be thrown onto the fires of purity, I know, and I know too there is no reward in being blunt, which Jay understood, as did Jim.

For speaking truth, they knew, feeling the direction of the wind on their white balding heads, only punishment.

THE HOUSEHUSBAND IV

He hated people who could not live up to Nietzsche words about 'suffering hunger in the spirit for the sake of the truth'

- Musil

One day all books will be kindling, warmth for small fires of survival at the end brought on by racism against white men, as prophesied long ago by Heidegger's pupil.

That is not a controversial position. The most open-minded know that every book ever created was birthed from the incestuous threesome of vanity, ignorance, and commercialism.

Vanity first, that psychotic megalomania must glow so strong in a man that he pours out a magma of his ego into the world. Ignorance too, no thinker ever gave us the whole truth, and for those who spoke as if they did, how much more ignorant they were, their assurance made them fools. Commercialism is critical, at last, that engine which creates sycophants who will defend anything a vain, ignorant writer says in any venue, on any subject, forever.

Today, in pursuit of being rewarded for my megalomania, I emailed a professor back at my graduate school in the cold black city of death, bewailing my position of having no position. I emailed a Jewish woman. She always wanted to be the mom in our cohort of pathetic rivals, the unifying figure. Perfectly, she always sided with the bullies.

Hypocrites like that Jewish woman in my cohort pretend they do not want to burn books, when they would burn every word ever written in the blink of an eye, if it meant they would gain. What I mean to say is save mine from the pyre, Important Creatives, and please show them to my mother first, as my philosophy is we must embarrass ourselves into fame.

A Masculine Trilemma

It was said that fiction writers should read philosophy '*but not too much.*' If a fiction writer is interested in the discipline, they should pursue that. I disagree with the blond novelist who perished on a motorcycle. Fiction writers should only read philosophy, history, religion. No good fiction now, only activism camouflaged, and the camouflage is not effective, like a fig leaf over an elephant's member.

Reborn in the sweaty flesh of an elephant's sex, I preach from before a cheap Target desk the obvious, I say what everyone knows: *there is no good fiction now*, only messages meant to engender power.

I wish I did not have these opinions. In these racist suburbs I am cold, and tired, thinking how 'death should not be feared because it involves our non-existence.' And now of the German philosopher, ruing his celebrity coming so late, and what can he do with it, being so old.

Schopenhauer also said women were Philistines.

Men are too, I know before a cheap Target desk, as I just scrolled on my phone and found a thonged fitness influencer, turning before her bathroom mirror.

To exist is to be racist, because I revel in how the influencer is ample, her two round cakes are like white clouds.

THE HOUSEHUSBAND V

Then will I wander god-like and victorious
through the ruins of the world
And, giving my words an active force,
I will feel equal to the Creator
                                                        -Marx

Baldwin and Morrison wrote hate. That is bad to say, I know, but bad is all I can manage in these racist suburbs, full of distaste for my white neighbors, whose children, full of snot, prance into our backyard to fetch filthy toys.

My eyelash flutters.

Near this unfurnished room, our white neighbors park their hybrid SUVs, in muted colors and bland shapes, close to our bedroom window. Nothing fits in their brown garage, bursting with plastic toys and boxes of memories they should burn.

I despise our unfeeling neighbors, not for their whiteness, but for their callousness.

Christ, now my cup overflows: one of the feral children just kicked a soccer ball in our backyard.

Why? I ask before a cheap Target desk in a bare room. That white child will work at a marketing job after college. If lucky, if the State has not commandeered all property, she will marry and buy a house in an adjunct suburb and only achieve in living further away from the cold black city of death.

When I lived there, a professor, Dick, gave me his copy of *The Town and the City*. Flattered, at first, that Dick would offer his copy. Later, I knew with a falling in my stomach, Dick gave me *The Town and the City* because he wanted to be rid of me. I hectored him too much with my wanting, giving him two full manuscripts of my unpublished work. Dick knew how long it would take to read that novel, the personal kind a man could once write and gain fame.

This obscurity is killing me, I think now, ruminating over a tip for delivery in these racist suburbs. My life has been reduced to worrying I did not tip enough for food deliveries, eating with my wife on her days off, coming to this cheap Target desk that she uses to work from home most days, going online to look up obscure authors, putting them in my cart, not buying most, receiving a few some days later, piling them in a corner of this house in the racist suburbs, never reading but hoping, by having more, I will become more, of something.

Why? No one is here but my wife and my child, and we are always inside, imprisoned after a color revolution using paid youth to create more power for the powerful. Nothing is free in this time where our lords of the virus relax on tropical beaches, and I dream of something I can never have as the world spins off its axis from too much corruption.

In young manhood, I can say from before a cheap Target desk, I did not believe the world was so broken. Even if that is what I was always claiming, as a houseparent in Nebraska, at a group home in Sioux Falls, that the world was *broken*, that we are all *broken*. By accepting Christ's sacrifice, I really told strangers in Colorado, we are *made whole*.

Now I am only made whole by getting out my phone, searching 'tanlines,' and finding someone robust yet *too innocent* to be on all fours, as the video's title claimed, slapped so that her round backside wobbles. I searched for her, I think now, to find a more lasting religion.

As there is no refuge in the one preaching that all who look like me must be burned alive. That theocracy says it is good to punish anyone who dissents. I just cannot assent to the new religion. The practitioners pray to false power, as the only god is the tanlined one whose backside was *too innocent* for that, yet she took what was given, as that is the dream, I believe as a househusband, to be with the one who does not appear to have been with many, and when they are with you they break their tether and are free to explore, to be explored, the tanlined Überwomensch.

Yes, the happiness of man is 'I will,' while the happiness of woman is 'he will.' Expressing our attraction is to make the speaker of that truth a degenerate, but I have nothing to lose in the racist suburbs, putting down these lust ravings for no one, with the goal being to excoriate those who peddle a worldview that says *something good will happen*, as long as one keeps doing 'the work.'

That kind of babble is what my graduate school professor, Jim, a self-proclaimed 'big fan' of Baldwin and Morrison, always preached.

Before this summer I did not see the way to solidarity. Now, I do. The only way we will find it is by banishing Jim, and those like Jim who their whole lives ignored anyone with real pains, as to entertain those pains would have meant becoming sincere, even vulnerable, to the plight of others, making themselves vulnerable, which people like Jim are too weak to be, vulnerable.

Now, again, before returning to my wife and child, I think of the tanlined one and feel heavy, knowing there is too we cannot have which we must carry with us. A yoke of wanting.

THE HOUSEHUSBAND VI

> You sow hemlock,
> and expect to see ears of corn ripen
> - *Machiavelli*

Wife and child in the kitchen baking wholesome cookies and I am before a cheap Target desk in a bare room, knowing we now live in a world where every serious book review must assert that the most essential element in any work of art are the immutable characteristics of its author. As I just saw one reviewer declare: '...it is easier to be white, obviously.'

Before this cheap Target desk, I know that reviewer should be spanked until admitting, *in this country*, life is easier for him, his bottom reddened, until he squeals, 'Yes, it is true, I am considered when it comes time to consider. I shine like a diamond of color, in the pile of *whiteness*.'

That neverchastened man, in another review, discloses his favorite novels. Imagine what a YA author would pick as their favorites, and that is his. YA is bringing the death of literature, I mean to say, and I am glad, as now a reviewer can write, 'it was never a good idea to write a book with only white people' and be praised. That reviewer should be jailed, I think, which now makes me the hypocrite. As if I say that reviewer should be jailed for what he thinks, I am being *for* progress.

What would not be hypocritical to say is how much I appreciate a Spanish beach handballer, sweating with frizzy hair under the hot sun, backside moving with power as she lunges in the sand. There are YouTube channels devoted to her and her sporty teammates, and those channels are more artful than any modern novel.

That reviewer would respond to my talk of the Spanish beach handballers by saying I am *a misogynist, and a racist*, as that is how that he copes, by calling what he does not know names.

The only good thing left for me to do, wife and child in the kitchen baking wholesome cookies, is to become meat for housewives. I walk by their quiet houses this summer of the planned virus in these racist suburbs. In good meat shape, I imagine, with strong legs and a flat stomach, those lonely, overworked wives would put away their water bottles and yoga mats, take down their stretch pants to the ankles, reach down to the thought of me dropping off my sleeping baby in their foyer, going to them wordlessly, turning them around and taking them in their kitchen, while their children play in the backyard, their husband working from home in the bedroom above.

Fantasy is all I have left. The rest is chores, joining social media, so I can be a Nazi, who says we should eject from society the racist reviewers of novels for formerly renowned arts magazines. As a Nazi, if I did not have my househusband duties, I would write three essays I should have written in graduate school. Their titles:

"We Exist Because of The Male Gaze"

"The Only Resistance is Against the Resistance"

"Thickness: An Argument for Lurid Art."

Instead I wrote soft dung, pleading for validation, and in the process I opened myself up to criticism from the oppressors who said they were the most oppressed.

Those people in my graduate school were bullied in junior high, bottled up their pain, until they found a way to release it through the assertion that they cannot be wrong, because of their *intersectionality*. Their way of getting back at the world was by enforcing what can be expressed. My limp nonfiction workshop professor was one of their enablers.

A Masculine Trilemma

In a meeting in his office once, he told me he was not 'easily offended.' This was after I worried I offended him in class, referencing too glibly, too *archly*, as he said, his former teacher in one of my essays. The limp professor was triggered in class, I knew, by the way he hissed in front of everyone:

'I *knew* John Gardner.'

The limp professor said otherwise in his office, though I could see through his clenched teeth he was shaken, decades later, by the man poets who visited his liberal arts college. Those man poets had whatever freshman they wanted, because they were kings then.

Now poets are inquisitors, like the people in my nonfiction workshop where I wrote feeble essays.

But nothing can be changed in the racist suburbs, where I am convicted, if I did the same as the German philosopher and submitted my essay to a jury for a prize, and I was the only who submitted my work, I would not win, as I am not serious enough, after going to my phone and searching 'pawg,' 'underarm hair,' and 'plowcam.' I clicked on the titles, have them waiting, and I know this will end with cleaning the wood floor and wishing for death, so I can be released from the prison of wanting to be Jeffers or Hamsun and being me.

I will only add, before going into my phone, decades before the virus and its subsequent color revolution for power, Rustin was arrested for protesting injustice. But we do not praise Rustin. We must praise the racist reviewers of novels for once regarded literary magazines. We must bow before the ransacking of cities. That destruction does the most for 'Black and Brown bodies,' as we are told.

We are told a great many things.

THE HOUSEHUSBAND VII

The destruction of the past is perhaps the greatest of all crimes
- Weil

From before this cheap Target desk I just read: 'A considerable number of countries, for about a hundred years, have enjoyed a practically complete freedom of public discussion, that freedom is now suppressed and replaced with a compulsion to coordinate speech with such views as the government believes to be expedient, or holds in all seriousness.'

Then I watched a video: of Paglia in the early 90s. In an interview, Paglia is shown a clip of a student of Strauss's who claims she has never heard of Paglia. Directly after watching the clip, Paglia laughs, dismisses the claim as a lie, and says with a flair, 'I am the Sontag of the 90s.'

Now viral teens make up our cultural soul, and I am glad for our new thought leaders. I believe, if our courage is this weak, we deserve the teens' sermons on who should be burned alive and who should be *stanned*.

Sontag, as is known, was not a nice person. So are 99.9% of all known writers, which is how you become a known writer, I have learned, by being an asshole, or by licking them.

I yearn to be the licker. For my literary climb I would choose a *Los Angeles Apparel* model (her mother is an important literary agent, I imagine) who attends the University of Chicago. During summer break my muse wears a white one-piece swimsuit, showing off thigh creases and underarm hair, which, I learn as a known man of letters after she has spoken with her mom about getting my book published, matches the rest of her.

Strauss taught young women like I one dream of. Sontag was one in the 50s, as was Sontag's girlfriend, who looked like the private college prototype, with bangs and the heart-shaped face. I will never be queer like them, and I take no comfort in my immutables, only in teens dictating our laws, and being able to judge a book by its cover.

Easily recognized, even a househusband before a cheap Target desk can spot them. A figure melting into a bird, or an abstract shape becoming the sun, all of it baked into a mushy color wheel appealing to aging, educated women, as cereal boxes appeal to children.

Baby sleeping, my housewife duties paused, I sit before a cheap Target desk thinking of what was said: 'Masculine republics give way to feminine democracies, and feminine democracies give way to tyranny.'

When I gave that quote last night, my wife said I should like Aristotle, as he championed free will. He said it was the only thing that distinguishes us from the animals. My wife knows things, she is a healer, I am only a househusband.

I say *only* not to demean housewives but to highlight how I am an obscure man of lusts with no hope, which makes me think of: 'Not to be born at all would be the best thing for man, never to behold the sun's scorching rays; but if one is born, then one is to press as quickly as possible to the portals of Hades, and rest there under the earth.'

Truer now, suicide rates rise for men, and it just as terrible for aging, educated women, drowning in news, no longer receiving the attention they did in youth and so they have convinced themselves, to pass their remaining years in a state of constantly being correct, the only god is the god of progress.

Women are not attractive after the age of 28, the German philosopher believed. My wife would say I would lower that age to 25.

And it is true, the private college graduates were that age when I tasted their ripeness. That odor was a trick of nature, I know in these racist suburbs, and am now glad to have been broken, as those private college graduates have matured into aging, educated women who would tire me out

127

with their regurgitated views on inequality and their petty gossips about work as a lawyer at a nonprofit.

Before a cheap Target desk, I wait for texts from the grocery boy, as I think of Diogenes in his tub. A good life, I believe now, to be warm under the sun, eating fish, drinking cheap wine, not worrying if your sacks of coin used as a pillow are taken.

The tech lords out in Mountain View (those men in charge of the viral teens) want us to think of them as modern Diogeneses. How absurd that is, seeing the tech lords testify before congress in frocks and nose rings and scraggly bears. Those drab outfits are meant to make us think the tech lords are poor in spirit.

Nothing could be farther from the truth.

Build bunkers, buy islands, freeze DNA, survive as long as I can, as the tech lords do?

For the privilege, it must be, to browse a library so big it would make Alexander weep, overflowing with brightly colored novels all with this moral:

'Be ashamed, white man, for you have been born.'

THE HOUSEHUSBAND VIII

Fuck Coltrane and music and clouds drifting in the sky
fuck the sea and trees and the sky and birds
-Knight

Now in the time of mandatory staying home I sit before a cheap Target desk and sing the praises of a woman before a bookcase riding a stationary bicycle on a modified seat (phallus attached). She wears only a t-shirt, showing her dedication to the art, and makes me despair. She pierces my gut. As was said: 'Happiness is only a dream and pain is real...I have experienced this for eighty years.'

Hounded by my coming years I sit alone (wife and baby in the basement of this ranch house in the racist suburbs) and witness a woman with muscular legs ride her stationary bike as if she does real exercise.

I have an I-It relationship to this woman, not an I-Thou, which is why I am in this solitary, bare room. Never have I had a threesome, I mean to say, and that pulling away from is what crucifies me before a cheap Target desk, time forcing me to know my greatest chances recede. Our prospects only decrease, I say. They fold, making the pleats of our own curtain of death, shrinking us away from the athletic woman who rides her stationary bike. The collapsing of society does not help, all these democracies claiming they want to save everyone from the grave.

My weakness is my almost threesome was closer to a decade ago than not and I cannot undo a moment which has estranged me from what would have been mine or any man's greatest accomplishment: that is, to engender enough affection in two women that they would battle with each other for reproductive supremacy.

129

A decade ago, I should say again, I lived with Hannah and Elena for a month. I held their Christian thighs every night. Blanket over us as we watched British television on Elena's laptop, in a living room in Madrona with the unused fireplace and filled built-in bookshelves. This was before heading back to the Middle West, after I had quit my dead-end job at the package delivery company and left the basement of a gamer landlord in Beacon Hill who played *World of Warcraft* all day. Every month or so, I admit, I went upstairs to steal her vacuum cleaner. That gamer landlord must have known I used her vacuum cleaner for my carpeted bedroom. She never said. She only yelled down if I made too much noise, like when I knocked my razor against the sink. That gamer landlord hated me, or pitied me, after I gave her my first manuscript and told her it was my 'whole heart.' She told me, when I meekly gave it to her, she would pass it along to her friend, a literary agent at Sterling Lord, but never did I hear from my that gamer landlord again, so I sold my possessions (golf clubs, framed art prints, GameCube, etc) and moved into Hannah and Elena's basement. Greer, by then in Bellingham for college, was not coming back. Years before, at the beginning of Cascadia, was Greer, Elena and Hannah, and others. By moving back to the Middle West, I thought by leaving, I could suppress my mistakes.

Erasing our mistakes is an illusion, I know now before a cheap Target desk, time tricking us into believing we have made the best choice. Considering our position, we tell ourselves, it must have been. But time is boiling water, convincing us the temperature of our present is healthy.

Everyone was moving out of the city, anyway, I told myself, to exburb villages with Native American names, and I wasn't that young, I believed, though I was younger than I am now and now I would say a person of the age I was *is* young, which is the hallmark of every age, I think now in these racist suburbs, to present the previous as a more promising one.

A Masculine Trilemma

Anyway, I moved into Elena and Hannah's basement, into their downstairs room with a garden level window and empty closet. Down in that basement room I would be Hannah on occasion. Elena was at night, in her room, where she kept a paperback copy of *The Easter Parade*, a book I recommended to her, on her bedside table. A large window in her room looked out at the mossy life. Before sleeping, Elena would take off her glasses. Her form was like that of sculptures.

Early morning and Elena would get up, dress in carpenter jeans, tough t-shirt, hooded sweatshirt splattered with paint, heavy work boots, and go drink her morning coffee. As the sun hit Mt Rainer I would slip into Hannah's room across the hallway. Bed near the ground, light coming into her room with more windows, Hannah would open her covers. Always after we finished, she would get up saying we were being 'silly,' then ready herself for her job downtown, raising money for the poor.

They were not witches, though they did throw their food waste in baskets, as if they used the rotting stuff for spells. And maybe, I think now, if I had drunk their potions, I would have stayed in that green city, not have needed to move, would have never met the private college graduates in the rented attic, never wrote a self-published novel about them, or anything at all.

But we are what we are, I know in the racist suburbs. No sense in remembering anything.

THE HOUSEHUSBAND IX

The true function of the writer in relation to mankind is continually to say what most men think or feel without realizing it

- Lichtenberg

Creative writing now amounts to communicating, through verse or prose, how much the author hates straight white men. Whoever does that the most artfully, from the most *marginalized position,* wins the creative writing prizes.

Unlearning that truth is the only way to save me, as I was born guilty. Even if I never touched foot on a ship of bad colonialism, I am guilty, as I enjoy the writing of heterosexual men who were born with little melanin in their skin and a member between their legs. For my sins of noticing, I will be put below the blade. Set on fire first, if I go further and state my distaste for the work of Voung, Coates, etc, along with all bearded male equity writers with blue checkmarks, those praised for obfuscating their message of *hate* with their advertised message of *justice.* Federal agents will roam this nation, eradicating my kind, hunting me for being born attuned to the female form.

Like yesterday in this bare room I saw on my muted phone an unbelievable one on a bed, so I ran to the comments, hoping to see others similarly overwhelmed. Her figure pierced my gut, creating in me a batter of longing, stirred with the viscous syrup of lust. Unable to find her name, I was driven to despair. She was perfect, with bee-stung titties, a big round ass, and a dumb tattoo on her side. No one in the comments knew her name, so in desperation I liked the video. In doing so, I became the desirer. The brand is permanent, I know before a cheap Target desk, this wanting.

It was just, the way she on the bed answered the questions, given to her by an unseen man, about how she did her squats after her college

132

homework at night, and how she looked like those I knew after their years in Northfield and New Haven.

I blame myself for this, for thinking of the private college graduates I once knew and their affluent grandparents on the coast, somewhere in homes with shelves filled with books advocating for the redistribution of all wealth except for the wealth allowing them to pay for their granddaughter's exclusive schooling.

For a long time, I should add, I had the idea for a novel where at the beginning everyone kills themselves. I never will create that thing, I know, remembering it was my phase with Camus that gave me the idea, as even if I did find the will, I would become reviled with myself, sitting before a desk thinking of *scenes* and *characters* with *motivations*. Nothing is worse, I know before a cheap Target desk, than a man alone making himself smile with delight at the creations oozing from his brain.

Maybe when Plato was around and nymphets ate a gilded man's ass to ensure its cleanliness, art seemed a nice diversion to entertain the leisure class as they ate grapes fed by heavy-breasted milk maidens. But there are no milk maidens anymore, only ex-girlfriends with *OnlyFans* accounts, and the transaction is cold.

Hedonism has become digital, I try to think like McLuhan on this day of an election where I will not vote. A disinterest in civics will not create a vacuum for a totalitarian. It is our increase in interest which engenders a larger desire in the virus lords to create more obstacles in overthrowing their power.

Aron, as Bloom wrote, was the last of the liberals, and I too wish to be as concerned with responsibility as Aron was, not the theoretical kind of those who insist that anything Western is evil. I mean never vote.

No other reasonable way to engage, unless one writes in their candidate, though that is fraught. The write-in will fail, if the write-in is elected, as the write-in will become intoxicated with power, which emits as strong a scent as the ass of a female animal in heat, and there is no love there, only lust.

Yes, I could spend all day this never voting day by clicking on videos of sweating women with bushy eyebrows, big thighs, a healthy bush, why? Other than to give context to yesterday, while playing with my child, my wife working from home in this unfurnished room, I had the thought of writing my *big novel*, where the emotions are real but the facts not. For my big book, I imagine now before a cheap Target desk, the first scene is in a park, my character reads *Zibaldone*, the sun shining, and a woman, a private college graduate who does squats, walks by the main guy under the shade reading, I think now, *By the Shores of the Silver Lake*, and his attention is taken, as it is warm and this woman is in Lycra shorts, peach colored, and in the height of sun with her big strong ass and midriff and wire glasses and normal face appears ready to bring home liquor and German philosophy to her newest boyfriend.

That kind of story cannot be told anymore, I know, and that they are banned is a blessing, and so, in a way, I am blessed.

In other ways, I am not, like how I keep switching back to a well-formed woman in a swimsuit pretending to have stolen something for a video. I watch again and am pained, seeing the dimpled flesh around her inner thighs where she shaved and left behind imperfections.

I can never have her.

THE HOUSEHUSBAND X

Harmful literature is more useful than useful literature
- Zamyatin

Mexicans move in next door. Across the street, Mexicans. Behind us, Mexicans. Now next door, more Mexicans.

Do not mistake me. Mexicans make fine neighbors, as good as any other, likely better than our only white neighbors and their loud children. I only mention the increase in Mexicans to highlight my failure, of *whiteness*, as I cannot afford to live next to the whites with their front yard greengrocer signage advocating for violent peace.

Among Mexicans, I know the managerial class, of which Antifa is under its payroll, is the greatest threat to modernity. I also know the only good things are real things, like if a woman is athletic but a little soft and, on all fours, looking at the camera, the man behind her, his face not seen, and the woman is glad, her dark long hair falling over her head, to be smiling into a camera. No facts outside that do I know today, needing to return to my househusband duties, other than what was said:

'Seek the company of those who search for truth; run from those who have it.'

THE HOUSEHUSBAND XI

The corruption of man is followed by the corruption of language
- Emerson

Today, instead of thinking of the unique results of our *free and fair election*, I should be working on my big pastoral novel about growing up on the Great Plains. I do not, as I know it will end up being about masturbation and yearning, with no characters or dialogue, so I bide my time and wait for Nature to take me, and think of how I could be known, in another life. Survive a world war first, as Malaparte or Grossman.

But where is the next world war so often promised? Maybe, if every atom that is not with us is shown as against us, there will be a great reckoning, and if I can live through it, *then*, at last, I will have a story Important Creatives want. As it is, I have not submitted in years, knowing with certitude now that all creative work's merit is based on a writer's place within a hierarchy of suffering. I am too low, or too high, and that forestalls me, keeping my trepidation not a conspiracy.

I should not worry so much. Everything is fair. Advertisements tell us they are. Ads come from tech executives doing mushrooms in their luxury yurts in Myanmar. The tech executives believe the masses are stupid, and we are, giving money so the tech executives can take more acid camping trips to Afghanistan to sell more ads that tell us the system is becoming fairer and no virus lord has bad desire, only progress until every one of us has been exterminated.

Problem is, every attempt to comport this world's entropy into a lush new garden is hubris. Even after first hanging all the straight white men from the gallows, letting their corpses rot, using their entrails for fertilizer, even *then* a new Eden would not be recreated. Humans will be base, full of envy.

136

Worse still, once my kind is all killed and the famines begin, the tech executives will be unable to eat their gold. Their stocks of vegan nuggets will be deserted once they cannot find potable water or get their electric scooters running. The fey pallid ones cannot hunt or fish and will always require the finest toiletries to clean their pampered, sagging asses.

THE HOUSEHUSBAND XII

> You will pursue them, begging forgiveness
> They will not forgive you
> *-Berry*

As grow older we gain weight *in theory*. I say before a cheap Target desk we gain *being* weight, and that mass physically presses down on our ability to become anything other than what we are. Aging accrues an ontological gravity, loading our steps, narrowing our privilege.

As it is known, the only privilege is the privilege of beauty, for a woman. Strength or intelligence, for a man. Only those privileges attract a better mate. There is no privilege in being born a certain color or gender. Anyone saying otherwise asserts their *dialectical power*, which they will use to silence anyone claiming a greater disadvantage.

As we grow older, we gain weight, and we shed privilege in the process. With privilege, it is right, when young, to be arrogant. As was said in a seminar in Iowa, 'If you lose your arrogance too soon, you may merely replace it with vanity.' Long before Berryman, another said: '...anyone who does not see the vanity of the world is very vain himself.'

There was a point to all this, I once believed, and if you worked hard and tried your best, there would be a reward in Heaven. Now, instead of Pascal, I think of Berryman again, who said in a poem he would be going to Hell and that was fine since: 'Hell could not be worse than this.'

Berryman had a sense of humor that kept him going, that and his conquests of undergraduates. He never read his own poems to them, I imagine before a cheap Target desk. He read those intelligent girls Bryon and Shakespeare, Schwartz, Yeats, Crane, the men he knew, and Dunne, Leopardi, Holderin, and that was enough, I am sure.

A Masculine Trilemma

That makes me remember again the limp professor who said in our nonfiction workshop, a grudge in his voice, that all those man poets acted 'like kings' when they came to his private college campus, long ago. Now that limp professor snivels, as he did in our workshop, that all men in literature should be 'forced out of power.' And especially, as he said, 'in the academic structure.'

That limp professor would never volunteer to be taken out first. He would hide behind braver souls, like the man poets who came to his private college in the late 60s and likely bedded his college girlfriend.

What I mean is this: male poets are not masculine anymore. There are no masculine heterosexual male poets, only banished, cowering worms.

THE HOUSEHUSBAND XIII

She'll say, compared with mine Callimachus's
Poems are rough---I like her liking me
                                    -Ovid

When I lived near a statue of Lenin, back in the middle aughts, I once sat in my white Taurus, parked on the street against the traffic, and, I thought on that misty day in Frellard, down the hill from a convenience store where every morning I bought a 20oz Coke and a king size Kit-Kat as energy for my *important novel work*, after my real work from 4AM to 8AM at my job loading packages for Company X, as I called UPS in the novel I was writing, I thought in my white Taurus, about to drive to Shilshole or Elliot Bay for my day job of waxing and cleaning yachts:

'Crazy, I'm going to be a novelist, crazy. People in real cities are going to know me as a *creative man*.'

So material and distinct, that memory, the feeling comes up all this time later, the excitement of knowing one will reach a dream.

In my white Taurus on another day, I remember from before a cheap Target desk, I talked with Jason. The sky darker that day, my hope of being known came with less valence, something was diminished. Not entirely was I decimated in Cascadia, but something once obvious about the future had become a less robust version. That uplifting feeling could no longer be conjured by simply imagining. My bubbling hope, not as effervescent, after sending manila envelopes of my *big novel* to Manhattan zip codes. I remember, the bearded Ballard post office worker that day acted like he knew what I was doing, asking me if I were sending 'manuscripts to agents.'

Sheepishly I said yes, and as I left the post office I pictured the worker receiving a daily harvest of envelopes from guys who like me, all of us similar in physiognomy, all of us looking to be recognized for transforming our heartbreak into art.

After that trip to the post office, and the subsequent rejections trickling in over the next months, I called Jason on that street in Frellard after my day of jobs. In my white Taurus, call on my flip phone over, I remember I thought I should have known Jason would tell me that after asking him advice on what direction I should take with my writing, since so many agents and presses said no, one even replying: '…stop writing immediately.'

Call over, in my white Taurus, I knew I should have expected nothing else from my former editor, a postmodern Christian who had turned into a polyamorous head of an arts magazine that made no money. Instead of 'We'll publish your stuff in our mag for now, man,' Jason said, '…look to the classics, man, the Greeks and shit,' as that is where I would find the inspiration to 'one day' find the 'necessary framework' for my stories about finding and losing the love of my life, a volleyball player from Iowa.

Jason used the phrase 'Hegelian dialectic' in conversations with every female stranger, I remember now. If that did not do the trick, he would say something that would make her feel *lesser than*. And I think now, I should have told Jason I was not calling for a lesson on the Greeks. I was looking to be known in this century, and I wanted, by being published in his arts magazine, to be known at parties alongside other pretend communists, I was a guy to look up to, as I had been published in a known arts magazine, so girls who built houses after private college could look at me and want. That's what I should have told Jason. I think I said something like, 'You're right, man, I *should* do that.'

Younger then, though not so young to be so ignorant, as I was, to the statue. Now the child terrorists in black, fighting for progress by setting buildings on fire, say they love Stalin, the murderer, who loved Lenin, who ordered killings, who loved Marx, who loved Hegel. Schopenhauer despised

141

the writing of Hegel, which Schopenhauer framed as, to quote Shakespeare, 'such stuff as madmen tongue and brain not.'

Child terrorists in black setting buildings on fire, forming mobs and infiltrating residential neighbors to intimidate citizens into obeisance, throwing paint on old women for progress, are the epitome of brain not.

I have no guns or armor to fight them in Portland, or elsewhere. No rations or medical supplies, only hate for people like Jason. As a househusband I will do my best to protect my family in the war against those like Jason and their minders.

'All men seek happiness,' as was said. 'This is without exception…This is the motive of every action of every man, even of those who hang themselves.'

A bigger worry than my suicide is not the child terrorists in Portland, but the drones and the jets above them. Power in controlling those death instruments comes in being able to blackmail men like me into feeling guilty for being born.

The only bad thing is, with a new war, I will never write my pastoral novel. Without it, I know as a househusband, there will be gnashing of teeth when the war begins again, this time for equity, as our virus lords want to comport me to say, so I may be *morally correct.*

So easy for the virus lords to preach. They have more than all the Caesars and Pharaohs combined, why not say the sin of being born the wrong way is progress?

But for me, this *O Pioneers* mixed with *The Magic Mountain*, this *Black Speak Speaks* with *In Search of Lost Time*, this *Little House on the Prairie* with *The Man Without Qualities*, who will write it, if not me? No one else will tell of the first time with Melody Fountains in her Sioux Falls apartment. Melody Fountains with in-between skin, light and dark, a swirling of athletic and thick, I knelled before her as she held the popcorn at the doorway of her kitchen, her gray sweatpants pushed down.

Maybe, if I apologize for being born the wrong way, the arbiters of what may be expressed will publish my story about Melody, and I would be so lucky, to be without testicles, flagellated, bleeding, published.

As the Important Creatives tell us, the more melanin in someone, the more rectitude, so I must pay fealty to the Important Creatives and their child terrorists stomping black boots. Never banished, only ever unknown, I have gone to the pamphleteer phase of my uncareer. Céline went to war first. He then came home and lay with shopgirls with defined clefts in their barmaid skirts. Not so obscene as de Sade or as affected as Huysmans, Céline was quotidian yet modern, and I mention those things to make it seem like that is me too.

Thinking of Céline and the quote I just read from Solzhenitsyn leads me to find that Solzhenitsyn met Putin, which is more depressing than the quote I read about the horror in Siberia, that Solzhenitsyn would perdure torture only to meet with a new Stalin named Putin.

Ah, but that's trite. Stalin was responsible for the death of millions, while Putin is not even as bad as federal agencies in this country. What I mean is never exaggerate. Never equate cruelties of the past with grievances of the present.

THE HOUSEHUSBAND XIV

> Girls
> First time a white man
> opens his fly like a good thing
> we'll just laugh, laugh real loud my
> black women
>   *-Clifton*

A dream last night of Greer. Dreaming a new *Aeneid* would have been useful. I dreamed of Greer, again.

Christ, I cry out to You from before a cheap Target desk and ask why we never dream anything but wisps which make us long for the dream that is not and lament the reality which is.

I dreamed of Greer, not the new *Divine Comedy*. To have dreamed a new *Cantos* could have helped.

Wife and baby nap, I do not know what to say of dreams or anything. No need for my stories. I cannot muster the energy, cannot start anything, as I would only receive silence. I dry these pathetic eyes to say a serious writer should keep writing his life story until he dies, and at the start of his book should be passages, one from Kafka saying how watching actors act out his work made him know all his words for them were false, and another from Kierkegaard saying how a typo from an author's work can become sentient and act as a living representation for how terrible the writer who breathed him into existence really is.

Yes, I believe before a cheap Target desk, a serious writer should only have epigraphs discouraging other writers, which was the goal, I think, for the most famous writer of the 20th century. He went into hiding after seeing the nature of things, and devoted his life to discouraging others from doing what he did and never doing it again himself, or, at least, if the disease was incurable and he did continue, he used the power he gained by ensuring not a word he did not want read was ever read.

My thesis advisor, Dick, liked Salinger, I think. I know nothing about my thesis advisor, really. Sometimes, I wish I had been an attractive woman in graduate school. If Dick had wanted to see my nice body, he would have found a way to publish me. But my ass is hairy, not wanted by the last straight male professors, those already fading into the past.

In youth, I liked Salinger. Now I only like Lamentations, the sermons of Menno Simmons, Murray race essays, Céline's pamphlets, Fallingwater, Kenkō writing about leering at plump washing women and losing his magic powers at 40, Apollinaire comparing his heavy heart to a Damascan woman's ass, Gombrowicz boasting that Kant, Schopenhauer, and Nietzsche were Polish, the art of thick thighs by Kacere, Harukawa, Modigliani, Frazetta, Courbet, Böcklin, Bouguereau, the recreation of Ruben's "Three Graces" by Saty & Pratha, the thinking of Rustin, the idea that perfection is oppressive as given in Rohmer's *Pauline at the Beach*, Disney films made before 1980, *Sherman's March*, the luridness of *Blue is the Warmest Color*, the impossibility of *Milo & Otis*, knowing *Inherent Vice* is PT Anderson's best film, *Bikini Car Wash* and other great 'Up All Night' on U.S.A. work, the pursuit of making art as highlighted by Borchardt in *American Movie*, the bean-shaped women drawn by Crumb, and Venus, who was callipygian in form, as well as never idealizing politicians, writing with chalk on a blackboard, the masculine films of Peckinpah, and the funny verses from Clifton about laughing at white men's penises. Nothing else. There is so little to enjoy.

All enjoyment is an illusion, anyway. As was said: 'Where did Dante find the materials for his Inferno if not from this world?'

Authors do not have to look long for the horrific, I believe in the racist suburbs. To find something positive is what is difficult. Easy to affect

145

an optimistic attitude in books where the world bends toward utopia if *certain parameters* are put in place, *certain legislators* voted into power, *certain corporations* given freedom to enforce their religion of all is political upon its workers.

Weak like the masses, I wear a mask at the grocery store like the other brainwashed cows. I kowtow when personalities say, 'The pandemic is real,' as I am ready to be taken, ravaged, by anyone who will publish me, after I correctly pronounce *incontrovertible*.

The stumbling happened. I was trying to point out to my mom the hypocrisies of our modern lords who mandate citizens stay at home, under curfew, with masks on their face, while those same lords do not stay at home, under curfew, with masks on their face, and we are supposed take these people as beacons of goodness, as lights toward which we should aspire, and 'all of it is given as *incontrovertible* truth.'

My mom, addicted to cable news, replied to say that *incontrovertible* sounds like 'a big word,' and I tried to say it again over the phone, and I did better, I think, but the moment was gone.

Aborted in the womb, I should have been, yet there I was, attempting to get a point across, and failing. I mention that interaction from the other day because I think every author should admit this: they should have been aborted but they were not, so they strove against their better state, of not existing.

This is getting bleak.

As was said: 'I do not believe in nonerotic philosophy. I do not trust any desexualixed idea' so I will relay the rest of my dream with Greer. Later in it I become a Persian king with good-bushed concubines, and my wife was fine with my needs when the wine flowed freely. As I told her in the dream, quoting another:

'The kings of Persia were wont to invite their wives to join them in their banquets; but when the wine began to excite them in good earnest and

146

they felt impelled to give the reins to sensuality, they sent them away to their private apartments, that they might not make them partake of their immoderate lust, and caused other women to come in their stead, toward whom they did not feel such an obligation of respect.'

THE HOUSEHUSBAND XV

Why these things and not other things?
-Beaumarchais

In this summer of the planned virus I saw them, three former presidents, lining up for *science*, they claimed. And to witness three former presidents servile like that only emboldens those who do not trust what they will be required to put into their plebeian veins.

Best that could happen now for the commoners is they get to live in society. The worst? The forced medicine propels us huddled masses further away from the closest needle as poor magnets zooming away from a colossal iron fist.

As it is known, what those three former presidents put into their blood was not the vaccine but a placebo meant to placate the unrich needed to lift up the world like Atlas, until the fantasy of the virus lord class materializes:

No underclasses, just the nobles, and robots serving the nobles.

Marx wanted to be God, which, I should admit, is a lot of us. It is just, a lot of us do not seek to compel everyone else to go out and make for them a heaven on earth, as those who pay lip service to Marx do now.

I should temper my public-school thoughts on political philosophers, I know. I always struggle to tap into the vessel of life by reading the great thinkers' explanations of the meaning of our blood. Wittgenstein would say that is impossible, to explain anything with language. *I think* he would say that. Anyway, to repeat, '...I do not trust any desexualixed idea,' I can say that even watching a compilation of shaking does not excite me.

Even with her on silent, I know I would rather have her, those like her, with tasteful tattoos, large asses, athletic thighs, to be in a more natural state, not Shakespearean in their ecstasy, more in a position which would make it easier to replace the man behind her, the star, and become the man myself.

With a normal performance, all can be done.

As the degenerate sociologist in Indiana reported, the average man goes about two minutes after initiating the act, while the woman can take up to fifteen minutes to reach a climax.

Christ should have made those apexes closer, I believe before a cheap Target desk, like with Hannah in Frellard. She reached hers like a man. Barely I would touch Hannah before she froze, her eyes rolled back, then came the shaking, the convulsing, the trembling. A hypothesis now, as a househusband before a cheap Target desk: Hannah wanted a boyfriend.

I never asked, moved on, and Hannah started dating a Boeing engineer, broke up with him, then she saw a flurry of guys, one of them a forester, I think. At some point she moved back to Madison and settled with a Steve, or maybe a Brad. Possibly, a Jeff.

Those I met in the frozen suburbs, the dark-haired private school graduates as red-haired Hannah, also had an easy way, so hair color must be a misleading trope and it is more that intelligent women who never thought they would be going to hell for feeling know better what gets them to the end and are more adept at closing the gap.

All in all, I think now in the racist suburbs, there are better things to do than smashing against one another.

Or there is not? Reading a book is digesting another man's vanity. Going into nature is fellating Christ's hubris, and what is trying to earn more other than making more for the lords of the virus who sell their expensive Tax the Rich sweatshirts?

Right now, below me in a drawer of this cheap Target desk, is the work of Kolakowski, and, I hope, by it being in a drawer below, its assiduity will seep into my veins.

I hope, I dream, I want, a life far from these racist suburbs, overrun with Jordans and Matthews, suffocating us with their Jordanness, their Matthewness. I should not judge. Those racist children will grow up wanting and never having, like their neighbor househusband who pretends he is a writer after three years of graduate school in the arts.

The point of that all was, I know now, to have an excuse for when parents called. Parents can be fooled, if their child is *furthering their education.*

Graduate school at an end, I know now, the point of expressing yourself is to get to where you are shamed. I know now, the difference between an interesting artist and an uninteresting one is the interesting artist's willingness to say that which will embarrass them.

Patterson and Oates know there is a war against my kind. What should get me killed is painting my dream life, far from these racist suburbs.

In a studio in the country, I imagine before a cheap Target desk, I paint naked pictures of Muhammad with his teen slaves. As I do, between my thighs are women a good decade or so older than Muhammad's, and my beefy-athletic harem, who look like they could play water polo for a living, do yoga for amusement, play video games in sheer underwear, and eat pancakes which make them a little heavy, while my wife is on vacation in her home country, and the Korean nanny watches the children in the main house. Back on the plains, my parents are glad to see their descendants grow strong, as they know, since I *furthered my education*, I am doing well.

And we are: my drawings of Muhammad are detailed, and I am paid well, so I have many athletic, intelligent women who cook pancakes over a small stove and wear thong underwear when they play video games. They kiss when they have mushroom tea in the forest behind my home in the country, far from modern governments who oppress the method I put pancakes on the table for my graces.

For imagining that azure life I will be imprisoned, and for imagining Liv, a body-building life coach with curly hair who takes pictures of herself in sheer underwear for her influencer social media. Her name is not Liv, likely it is Anne, or Liz, or something else befitting of Liv's plain face, tattooed back, muscular legs. I found Liv and will never know her, or that farm. That is my pain. My pain that is making me, wrongly, want to make more words exist.

Still there should be novels about how Anne, or Liz, or whatever Liv's real name is, can never be one of the 23-year-olds at my farm between my thighs and after work of being between my thighs she goes to play video games and eat pancakes in my studio. Feeling a little heavy, she walks into the forest to drink mushroom tea and there begins to explore the other ones on my farm. She lays on the fecund earth in the gloaming. On a wool blanket she feels other tender breath, receptive pink nipples, then I later come out to tell them 'I love these cold asses as much as I love your warm asses' when they lay before the TV in thong underwear after taking care of me as I draw my paintings of Muhammad.

THE HOUSEHUSBAND XVI

Truth has very few friends and those few are suicides
- Porchia

Every day upon waking I am asked, 'Will it will snow today?'

And I always debate whether to tell my truth, 'Honey, look at your phone yourself,' but I always stop, knowing saying such a thing will incur disputes, one tense passing in the hall of this house to another, so I always acquiesce to mustering, 'Not sure, I'll check,' though I am sure of the weather (as I have looked the night before). Or, I wonder now before a cheap Target desk, my wife simply wants someone else to be in charge of what she should wear that day, someone else making a decision, so she might have one fewer in a life where she has too many, working at a job that upholds the house, which is not the natural way of things, I know, but it is not 1850 in Paris, and I cannot be paid to write of big asses in the forest. No one has asked me to paint an angel and my response would not be: 'Show me an angel, and I will paint one.' I am only rotting meat in the racist suburbs, ignorant to how to enroll Spanish beach handballers with frizzy hair into my cult where we pray to a Gnostic God. I do not have a proper answer when my wife asks each morning if it will snow.

A successful man would. This man, who knows the histories of all religions after reading Eliade, says to his young bride, 'Woman, look on your phone, and never ask again about the weather, now go make breakfast,' and he spanks his young bride as she giddily goes, joyfully with pink areolas and a wobbling, athletic ass and thighs as alluring as the thighs Abe wrote about, the kind a successful husband would want to 'wrap all his nerve endings around,' to go make breakfast for her man who fulfills his evolutionary function.

No, I think before a cheap Target desk, I have no answer when I am asked each morning if it will snow. Carrying our baby in the living room, bouncing up and down and singing to him, I have no answers.

'Definitely won't,' I want to say.

'Why?' I imagine she replies.

'Because it never snows,' I dream I say. 'God does not send down His snows to us. He has moved to worlds where there are no colors. Never unhappy or happy, those worlds are neutral, and He is glad to have made those people not racist, or anything at all.'

That answer would put to rest the questions about the weather, I think.

Other than the nature of God, I can say with certainty this morning the only lame act in this life is to designate as lame that which you have not yet experienced.

Another thing, I am tired today after a night of our baby waking up to feed. A good poem would have that line: 'I am tired today,' and that alone would resonate.

To write a good poem would be nice, to spend my remaining moments trying to make one good poem for no one. Problem is, we need more poems as we need more Hitlers, Bidens, Sartres.

Spot them, perverts in charge who like to watch things burn. For destroying the world they want to be rewarded with young, attractive crops, and they believe the way to attract the ones with the kind of 'body at eighteen years to which nothing sufficiently blinding can be compared except the sun...'is to destroy in the name of the Colored man, or the caricature of the Colored man: holy, oppressed, in need of infinite help.

I know I should sleep now, yet I crave the new. I just do not have enough status to have them. No golden trophies to entice Spanish handball players. And still I have wantings, writings. No one says they need to exist.

No one would care if this vanished, not like if the work of Ellul or Weaver vanished. I have never read a book by Fanon or Lacan. I try to divide the world into my pain I understand and do not judge the pain of others I cannot.

Otherwise, before a cheap Target desk, I should say I deleted my Twitter again. *I look like I was kicked off,* I thought, at first, but now realize I am not prominent enough to be considered dangerous. Worse, I find every day I am losing pieces of my drive. Vanity would push me toward the finish, I once believed. Now, I think, there is no finish, more a pathetic shuffling off the track.

If I had to do it all over again, I would not. I would place my energies in physical labor. Also, I just checked, and I did not know my rejections were all so bland. I remember more 'send us more.' Time passing is a softener of suffering. My immutables should be changed, I know as the househusband, my innards should be cleansed with gasoline.

And still I want to go back to the Caucasus, and live in the mountains, with purple flowers spreading over cold meadows in early spring, a maiden with golden breasts, fleshy thighs, a dark triangle mound is there pulsing for the rejuvenation of her ignored body, as too many men have been told they should want another man.

Yes, to put this pure maiden in the cold meadow, warming with the sun, and show her the fullness of what a man is capable of, that is, to give her the manifestation of my pink maleness.

THE HOUSEHUSBAND XVII

Still ardent with the lust of her stiff vulva, she retires, weary of men yet still not satiated
- *Ariadne*

Overwhelmed now with *that feeling when*: the department chair of a creative writing graduate school program sends: 'an interesting call for pitches,' and that *interesting call* solicits the work of anyone: 'non-white.'

These days, after opening those sorts of emails, I dissociate, and become somewhere else, as someone else, Jeffers, perhaps, writing about a hawk above the coast of his stone house in Carmel, or Berryman smoking a cigarette on a cold walk through Powderhorn Park. I cannot imagine, I mean. I certainly cannot imagine I am non-white. That would make me the appropriator. In a 'creative double-bind,' as Nunez wrote, there will be nowhere to go but jail. Real jail, I mean before a cheap Target desk, for my thoughts, which will be confirmed righteous or stamped heretical by our lords. Democracies are farces, we know now.

No more than that do I know, listening to Lipa in headphones, to the video of her dancing in red shorts with tender meat in them. She wears a cutoff white t-shirt, has jumping pertness, and I think of the part where Darconville calls upon Isabella, and just Isabella saying 'present' makes Darconville go on a mediation of devotion invoking lighting, nature, and gods. Corralling these thoughts will be a way for our virus lords to attain more power, so they might more easily use children as slaves on private islands.

Stay quiet about the evil. My time would be better spent with family in the living room, while I am before a cheap Target desk, obsessing. Hölderlin was not known in his life, Diderot, Dickinson, Du Fu, but they at least had imagination. Mine funnels through a tiny hole, centered as a laser on the ongoing mass psychosis. No story here. No *Shoah* or *Satantango*, only a

155

househusband who recently finished graduate school trying to be known for his thoughts.

Would be better for him to retire to a cold corner of a ranch house in the racist suburbs and watch every episode of *Walker, Texas Ranger* until wasting into a pile of bones. Anything would be better than sitting here compiling discontent with how the world does not want the literary submissions of a straight white man.

Yesterday, I could say, I came across a guy who gave up on this pursuit in his mid-thirties. Now he reviews postmodern literature on YouTube. He gets a couple thousand views for each video. That kind of fame is more than I could dream of.

Driving myself into oblivion, all because I once lay with private college graduates in a rented attic. I must forget them. Those privileged ones were right not to sign up for a lifetime of expulsion onto their dark mounds then listening to a bald man in their curly hair talk, not about how much they learned at Carleton or Alfred, but about what a tragedy it is he is not glorified for his words.

'A human being comes,' a man wrote, 'and other things I cannot comprehend.'

What the coming is, I can remember, like the runner who graduated from Grinnell. She had nipples like thimbles, I once wrote, and, I thought in the frozen suburbs with her, *it will always be this easy*. She acted as my moon and more and I treated her like dust from a comet streaking across the sky of my existence, not realizing how chances could burn, how I could wake one morning on my mattress on the floor and realize: *Reality has overcome promise*, so I told her to go to another. At the time, in my elderly adolescence, I did not yet see the reality hidden behind the fantasy: I was a thing not to be brought home to parents.

A Masculine Trilemma

Not a bad boy, a bad *thing*, white, factory, rented attic and mattress on the floor, with no plans for more schooling other than my land grant undergraduate degree in psychology, which was like toilet paper to the parents of those private school graduates.

The next I met in that time told me to pull her soft dark hair, so I did. Weeks later, in my rented attic she said, on the mattress on the floor, 'I'm pregnant.'

'I'm joking,' she said right after, unpausing the movie, and I think I laughed. I tried to.

The funny joke is she would have been happy with my baby. That private college graduate told me to grow my hair out. She saw the best version of me, rejecting those who saw white, factory, rented attic and mattress on the floor.

Buber would have approved of our relationship. He and that private college graduate were in the same tribe, though Buber's point was that we are all one tribe. What I know for sure before a cheap Target desk is that young men who describe themselves as poets are too precious, while young men who describe themselves as essayists are too serious, and old men who call themselves novelists should be put down.

'The brain secretes thought as the stomach secretes gastric juice, the liver bile, and the kidneys urine.'

I agree, as those old men would be better off vomiting the electricity from their brain into an open field or the backyard of their ranch house in the racist suburbs paid for by their better half who supports their hobby of starting fires in a room then complaining the world does not appreciate these burns. At least our virus lords are transparent in their hunger. They want until there is one flame unifying all adulation toward them.

One should not stand up and do something, I must insist at last before a cheap Target desk. One must throw away their phone, cut bundles of wood

157

and make strong shelters. Hunt with bow and arrow the game of the field. Eat that meat and use animal hides for warmth. Never engage with those who would use your being as a cudgel for power.

If that is too much, do not complain. Be okay with hearing your modern lords say you are bad because of how you were born. Be satisfied with your leader being a decrepit man who gives himself senile titles.

Now is time for the second dawn of man, I mean, for anyone with tools for fire and hunting who does not want to listen again to blue-checked pawns disseminating hate to increase power for the powerful.

THE HOUSEHUSBAND XVIII

Convulsive beauty will be erotic, veiled, exploding-fixed, magic-circumstantial, or will not be at
all

- Breton

No skin color gives anyone privilege, I say before a cheap Target desk in the racist suburbs.

The only thing that matters is what side you are on.

If obsequious enough you will be granted liberty to speak, though it will not be your mind, if moral. As was said: 'Freedom only for supporters of government, only for members of a single party, however numerous---this is not freedom. Freedom must always be for those who think differently.'

Freedom is now something for the lower classes to yearn after, a funny thing for those in power to laugh about. If lucky, the commoners may chew on freedom's last morsels which fall off the bloody bone deep throated by the lords of the virus class peddling their violent democracy across the world.

Kolakowski, who loved the historical thinking of Marx but thought Marx's theories incomplete, would not have great praise for my metaphors. He thought Marx left an opening for despotic rule by the proletariat, replacing capitalistic oppression with bureaucratic terror. I say all politics become religion. In these racist suburbs I want to indulge in another religion, capitalism, by purchasing first print editions of Hamsun's work.

For enduring one's self there should be a reward, as I am a glutton, for loving Maria, as was her name in the video I saw on my phone. Brown, with an unwaned backside spanked and handled, she made the viewer believe he should keep striving so one day he could make wobble her ass like two big apples, nutritious, firm, full of grand wobbling. All I really know in these racist suburbs is my happiness would come in never eating again, as I am thinking of submitting again to literary journals that do not want my work.

In that vein, this morning in the grocery story I overhead a white boy tell a black girl, teens in masks stocking shelves, something about Emmett Till, and I know the white boy said what he said to engender positive feelings in the black girl. Now, before a cheap Target desk, I hope that white boy sows good feelings in that black girl and they have swirled children and begin the dictatorship of the working class.

My favorite Marxists are the earnest ones, I mean to say, those who believed in strange wonders, who thought in terms of all or nothing, who wanted to institute a utopia where they would be free to have as many as they wanted and not be penalized, as there would be no real government, and every man would be glad to be in charge of their own team of Spanish beach handballers.

That was not Marx's plan. He thought we would need to work for a portion of the day. My vision is of Spanish beach handball players who set up camp in Exuma and eat jamón, brought in by a man who enjoys their big asses so sweaty from activity.

Houses? Electricity? We will not need to stare at our phones for affirmation, as there will be tan asses in small bikinis, playing sports and enjoying nature. Any other government causes the exploitation of man, as is the *nature of things.*

Me, a househusband, I live off the labor-value of others, thinking of a system, that if woven into social consciousness, would improve our *collective existence,* for me a field of Spanish beach handball players, college long jumpers or hurdlers, water polo players or softball players, engaged in healthy competition, all with noticeable wedgies of their nylon (who will make the nylon will be a discussion for another time) sporting bottoms, and they are picking those wedgies and slapping each other's tanlined asses on the beach, and I go out to get more jamón and casks for wine for the nightly feasts. The will of history leads us to this, my vision materializing now before a cheap Target desk.

Robespierre would agree, Fourier, Hubbard, Luxemburg, Lafargue, others I cannot remember, but I do not want to search anymore, tired of encountering my ignorance.

Someone fill my gaps, like in the video of Malkova, the original Venus, oiled and rubbed with a wand by an Asian man until she there are squeals of good pleasure, until puffy nipples show through a greased gossamer white bralette telling me I need to keep going so one day I can make myself have enough status that Malkova, or better yet her upcoming doppelganger, notices me after I upend the literary world with my works of masculine throbbing. For the first time in forever a literary man whose testosterone has not dipped can impregnate his wife, the worshipers in his sports harem, *and* his star, a younger Malkova.

I should cleanse myself, I think before a cheap Target desk, follow Christ, start a commune which shuns government meddling, as my Anabaptist grandfathers did with their brick church on the plains. That could be my human dawn with my younger Malkova, the ruddy princess, and my wife, the matriarch.

Quarrels, yes, but I would not be worn out like Hrothgar, I would be invigorated and settle their disagreements until we understood this was for the betterment, this community on the prairie isolated like the Hutterites, where we never restrict, where let it all come as Breton dreamed, and my peaceful valley has two commandments to follow, as the Jews followed theirs and were led to the milk and honey in Canaan, our rules are simple in this place with the warm breezes, clean sunshine, and hearty fires in winter:

Do unto others as you would have them to do unto you.

Do not censor yourself.

161

And you can see it now, my worshipers in various undress down in the valley, cleaning each other in the washing creek, letting the chilly water prick their hearts and pink nipples with the invigoration of freedom.

THE HOUSEHUSBAND XIV

With purity and with holiness I will pass my life and practice my Art
-*Hippocrates*

No more thoughts of the private college graduates, Christ, please. Even if we met again, after our entwining, head in their hairy laps, I would say something defeatist about how I found Krzhizhanovsky to be analogous, not in his work's strangeness, but in how I will not be read while alive, and that I would like to be with many others with genuine smiles and athletic bodies, natural hair put into a bundle and pulled, so the well-raised, curly-haired, privileged head is reared back like a bucking horse.

Christ, I know I should be doing taxes in these racist suburbs, or reading, or plowing the snow, not reveling in the plowing. I should be jumping from a bridge before my kind becomes illegal, that is, straight white men who publish their thoughts.

I believe before this cheap Target desk that Christ smote me at birth, giving me this desire. The curse He imbued in my being is the rushing that goes through before I can impart the *correct lashing* which the convex-tummied ones with thighs like trunks, desire. He banished me to racist suburbs where I should be doing taxes, or reading, or plowing the snow, but never the Spanish beach handballers with frizzy hair in a godly row. Complete silence, is really what I need. No more thumping beats from Perry. In silence, I might think of a divine way of living as Gurdjieff did. No more writing fiction no one buys.

No man buys, I mean, only aging white women, and I do not want to plunge into any aging white women, only Spanish beach handball players with fresher outlooks and higher asses.

For those women is my new religion, where instead of dancing like Gurdjieff to wake our consciousness, we use the release from our sober bodies, high on the clean air of the country, far from the managers, and yes sometimes we are elevated on flowers that give me, the lead guru, a detached mind, which helps keep me going through the ecstatic moment.

We would not dance to find nirvana, not a series of complicated movements to elevate the consciousness, our act would still be warm and eruptive, with feminine hands around the masculine mast, and our ship would have two simple commandments:

Do unto others as you would want done to you.

Do not censor yourself.

Yes, my religion would have a great deal of Spanish beach handballers, red bikini bottom riding up tan asses, coming over to the leader to give a tickling with frizzy hair, then swallowing well, to find *the way of learning.*

I mean to say, in these racist suburbs, I watch on my phone Spanish beach handball players play their games in opulent beaches, off the coast of France, on a remote island in the Caribbean, an island off Africa, and know I will never see my followers in real life. By the time I form my religion, our virus lords will have colonized those places and brought rule which will not allow a man to choose his life, like that of the religion of big round asses slamming against a leader, who is tall as a mast for the devotion.

No more fiction.

Fiction is for aging white women who want to feel guilty for how they were born, their bodies no longer able to do what the Spanish beach handballers can do.

No fiction. Only silence, though even silence is racist. Instead I should start a farm in paradise, grow a beard, and show intelligent, athletic women I have the answers they seek, that life does not have to be all usury and misery, a perpetual feed of rancor through screens meant to divide us into racist and moral.

First, I plan before a cheap Target desk, I will tell my robust followers this: delete everything, women of my flock, and keep going until nothing is left of you online, so that when the reapers come, your family will be able to say, 'No, police of equity, that brat is long gone, do not shoot at us with your guns of unity. That woman of sedition and insurrection had wrong ideas and does not exist.'

Nothing left to imagine in these racist suburbs.

Delete, until there is nothing the police of equity can find when they come knocking.

My family will be unimpeachable, and my Spanish beach handballers will gird our righteous fortress and we will not be meat at the human meat picnics. We will get up every morning and read our own holy scriptures. At night, after steak and beer, we will entwine. After entwining, restoring sleep, under the stars.

THE HOUSEHUSBAND XV

And all this, as said, not for the grace of God, nor out of loyalty to Kohlhaas, as to whose fate they were quite indifferent, but for a mask under which they might loot and burn to their hearts' desire

- von Kleist

In a building in West Allis (for a century they made heavy machinery there) I was with defeated others. In those remains I once sat in a cubicle, every day checking the portal reporting how many books I had sold of my first novel about online dating.

Every day in that cubicle I hoped, after promoting my work on social media and accruing likes from real women. I wrote then for a popular online magazine, stuffing itself with listicles about being a millennial.

No one is a millennial now. Only Zoomers, and I am glad for their coming reign. With Zoomers in charge no longer will I need to fool myself and submit to journals and wait on rejections. Those emails were always a ceremony, causing pain.

When I started this in Cascadia I sought to salve the pain of heartbreak, a volleyball player from Iowa. Through continuing about others and believing I deserved to be read for recounting their memory has increased the pain.

Now before a cheap Target desk there is the inner voice: *join social media*, reach out to RW publishers, now cropping up in reaction to the discrimination.

But I will be rejected by the men who have been rejected. They will say have not eaten enough raw eggs, or I did not read the correct version of the Bible. A defect will be found.

166

My wife tells me, after we move out of these racist suburbs and go to the north woods, I should open a bookstore. The other night in the kitchen I dipped my chip in salsa and replied, 'Yeah, maybe,' so she could think well of her man's future.

A day passes, and my hate increases. Yesterday afternoon a kid knocked, loud as the police, and I opened the front door of this house in the racist suburbs and a kid was there, making faces. My wife, holding our baby, asked from the green couch, 'What is happening?'

'There's a fucking kid here making faces,' I said. 'I think it's a game.'

The boy turned, ran gangly across the street, and there across the street joined up with his giggling friends.

Parents in that house made us into an I-It, so children are not scared to knock on our door and make faces. My hate for my white neighbors locks the idea for a story called 'Fairygasms,' a mix of Ballard and Spencer. The idea has crumbled, dissolved, washed away from the rain coming down in these racist suburbs. I do not live in a high-rise eating dog or have an epic adventure for a knight. I can only think of what I could do with my life now that we are moving, this time north, into the woods. My contributions there could not afford more than a hut.

My idea for a story about fairies coming will never happen, and now again I am thinking of that bookstore in West Allis, how it would be burned down. The protestors would throw their bricks of progress and Molotovs of inclusion and the police would arrest me for keeping in my store the books of authors to the right of Trotsky.

No bookstore in West Allis. No literary journal, *Polemics,* either. No one wants that, not even a journal conscripting the work of the black women I knew in graduate school who I admired for their bright spirits, free minds, impressive backsides.

The only way to be happy is to be secluded in the north woods and make videos reviewing my favorite books, which will end up being video criticisms of the world that will attract other discontents at the edges, those not lucky enough to be listening from their hut in the north woods but from a computer in a public library, or from the upper level of a duplex in a city run over by riots meant to tell everyone to put in the correct candidate.

Worse, I am a hypocrite, ready to be crushed by commerce at a distribution hub, ready for Chinese businessmen in masks and suits to stroll by my workstation while they have muted conversation, no one looking at me in the eye, as I would be a robot to these Chinese businessmen in the north woods, there at the distribution hub to examine production techniques in the factory which ate more of the land the original peoples lived on without disturbance.

For the Chinese businessman, it would not be racist for them to disturb the land. They have a little melanin. God save the red-headed pale women, moving up on the scale until we get to the humans with the darkest hue, who cannot sin.

The moral laws of the universe, as prescribed by our lords, must not be questioned.

In that spirit of truth and memory, I should remember how I once drove from Sioux Falls to Spokane in a day. Good things come to those who try, I believed in youth. Cowboys in Wyoming, endless Montana, white stars in the mountains above Idaho, my heart was full when I arrived in Washington state. Good things came that year in Cascadia, then they left and are now married to men who will never work at a distribution center carved out of nature by our rulers. What do I mean to say by recounting all this?

Just that I have come here to cry, and I have cried.

THE HOUSEHUSBAND XVI

When he touched my body,
couldn't at all remember
who he was,
who I was,
or how It was
                -Amarusataka

My favorites make me bad, and I must find peace in that. No time for worrying in these racist suburbs with things to do, like that journal of arts and culture with the black women, E and S and K, and I want to make videos on all the books I have read, and there is the fiction sent from my intersections of obscure and gentile in the chosen suburbs of the north woods. At the same time, I know, no editor in their right mind would read my words, and all editors are in their right mind, publishing the most daring work which never bows to our lords in control of the government, all major corporations, and every institution. For that gallant editor, I had the idea for a novel about an unchosen man's love of chosen big asses, full bushes, ripe mounds, thick thighs, curly hair, but before starting, I knew, the amount of energy expended for such a thing would not be commiserate.

Worse, I hate all new books.

The only thing that helps is the drinking water in these chosen suburbs.

All soda companies want my extinction, I know as the househusband, as soda companies believe promoting a certain kind of genocide will increase positive brand exposure.

Once, I believe, to protest the annihilation of a people because of how they were born would not have been a radical thing. I am not so radical, remembering rich chosen asses slapping on my poor unchosen cock.

That is crude, I know, though using prick makes it no better, and the matter at hand is not my anatomy, nor the drinking of water in protest of soda corporations promoting the genocide of a people based on their skin color, the matter at hand is my hatred of all new books, and that I insist on writing them.

Later, I know, when the dread of having no audience becomes too overwhelming, I will delete all this, then comes the relief.

'Each suffers his own torments.'

I pile them on, these aches of not knowing the knowing I want with the Spanish beach handballers or the private college undergraduates in my imaginary creative writing classroom.

With no beach or commune or office where my followers would be excited to know their leader, I am far away from those who worked their minds in high school and their bodies in college in water polo or handball, who kept themselves ready for a learned man, and this bereft state causes suffering, this vision of the water polo creative writing student in my seminar who loves Jeffers and more so loves how I quote Jeffers and she would be *really excited* to meet after class at a café and comes in meekly, fragrantly, wearing colored yoga pants I never saw her in before.

THE HOUSEHUSBAND XVII

All writing is pigshit
-Artaud

The sky grows dark. Wife and child away to the in-laws in the western suburbs, I do not know God, have only bad thoughts of joining social media again, of adding novels to a newsletter service. If I go ahead with the debasement, I will be no further than over a decade ago in the frozen suburbs, when I embedded my first attempt, *Lovers of Salvation*, into my personal website.

If I had died in Minneapolis, none of this. If between the CNC machine and the bed of cold-rolled steel I was gutted, I could have left this realm as potential. With hints of tragedy, maybe, if someone had squinted at my life at 33. The age Christ perished is when metal spikes would have impaled me. An unfeeling, mechanical motion stopping my heart, blood gushing onto the steel factory's concrete floor, as Steve, the rail-thin chain-smoking man who worked back there with Dean, hurried me out of the warehouse, while the other guys' last memory of me would have been my bleeding to death. Instead, Steve shouted, jumped over, pressed the emergency stop, and I slid out before the metal tines ended my breathing.

Whose fault was it? I am not sure, still. Maybe it was both of ours.

Steve, white as paper as I hopped out, said nothing for a minute or two. Eventually I think I laughed, the eerie brush of death gone, and Steve later managed a smirk. Never did I tell my family.

Then the other night in bed, unable to sleep in these north woods, I felt the weight of my trying, and it seemed so heavy I succumbed to a bout of solitary tears in the dark.

After a bit I controlled myself, embarrassment overcoming pain. Wiping away tears, all was quiet. Wife and child slept. The earth rotated slowly.